The Mother's Day Mishap
by

Kathi Daley

I want to thank the very talented Jessica Fischer for the cover art.

I so appreciate Bruce Curran, who is always ready and willing to answer my cyber questions; Jayme Maness for helping out with the book clubs; and Peggy Hyndman for helping sleuth out those pesky typos.

And, of course, thanks to the readers and bloggers in my life, who make doing what I do possible.

Thank you to Randy Ladenheim-Gil for the editing.

And a special thanks to Sharon Guagliardo, Pam Curran, Patty Liu, and Darla Taylor for submitting recipes.

And finally, I want to thank my husband Ken for allowing me time to write by taking care of everything else.

Books by Kathi Daley

Come for the murder, stay for the romance.

Zoe Donovan Cozy Mystery:

Halloween Hijinks
The Trouble With Turkeys
Christmas Crazy
Cupid's Curse
Big Bunny Bump-off
Beach Blanket Barbie
Maui Madness
Derby Divas
Haunted Hamlet
Turkeys, Tuxes, and Tabbies
Christmas Cozy
Alaskan Alliance
Matrimony Meltdown
Soul Surrender
Heavenly Honeymoon
Hopscotch Homicide
Ghostly Graveyard
Santa Sleuth
Shamrock Shenanigans
Kitten Kaboodle
Costume Catastrophe
Candy Cane Caper
Holiday Hangover
Easter Escapade
Camp Carter
Trick or Treason
Reindeer Roundup

Hippity Hoppity Homicide
Firework Fiasco – *June 2018*

Zimmerman Academy The New Normal
Ashton Falls Cozy Cookbook

Tj Jensen Paradise Lake Mysteries by Henery Press:

Pumpkins in Paradise
Snowmen in Paradise
Bikinis in Paradise
Christmas in Paradise
Puppies in Paradise
Halloween in Paradise
Treasure in Paradise
Fireworks in Paradise
Beaches in Paradise – *July 2018*

Whales and Tails Cozy Mystery:

Romeow and Juliet
The Mad Catter
Grimm's Furry Tail
Much Ado About Felines
Legend of Tabby Hollow
Cat of Christmas Past
A Tale of Two Tabbies
The Great Catsby
Count Catula
The Cat of Christmas Present
A Winter's Tail
The Taming of the Tabby
Frankencat
The Cat of Christmas Future

Farewell to Felines
The Cat of New Orleans – *June 2018*

Writers' Retreat Southern Seashore Mystery:
First Case
Second Look
Third Strike
Fourth Victim
Fifth Night
Sixth Cabin – *May 2018*

Rescue Alaska Paranormal Mystery:
Finding Justice
Finding Answers – *May 2018*

A Tess and Tilly Mystery:
The Christmas Letter
The Valentine Mystery
The Mother's Day Mishap

Sand and Sea Hawaiian Mystery:
Murder at Dolphin Bay
Murder at Sunrise Beach
Murder at the Witching Hour
Murder at Christmas
Murder at Turtle Cove
Murder at Water's Edge
Murder at Midnight

Seacliff High Mystery:

The Secret
The Curse
The Relic
The Conspiracy
The Grudge
The Shadow
The Haunting

Haunting by the Sea:

Homecoming by the Sea

Road to Christmas Romance:

Road to Christmas Past

Chapter 1

Thursday, May 3

They arrived in the middle of the night. Two balls of wet and matted fur tied to a porch railing, huddled together for warmth and comfort as the rain slammed into the small town of White Eagle, Montana, from the east. The note said they were inseparable, brothers who'd shared a womb and eventually a life. Neither had spent time without the other, and, the anonymous person who'd dropped them on Brady's doorstep asked, if at all possible, could they be placed together?

Placing dogs with just the right owner was a task Brady Baker, local veterinarian and shelter owner, and I, Tess Thomas, mail carrier and shelter volunteer, take great pride in doing better than anyone else, but this pair of medium-sized terriers were proving to be quite a challenge. It wasn't that they weren't adorable, with their huge brown eyes and long shaggy fur the color of damp sand; it was that they had never been trained or socialized to respond to or even care about anyone or anything other than each other.

And then they met Tilly.

"It looks like you're making progress."

Brady smiled in response to my statement as my golden retriever, Tilly, and I walked into the room where he'd been working on a sit/stay with one of the brothers. It appeared as if the training had been going well until Jagger saw Tilly. Ignoring Brady's command to stay, he'd run forward to greet her with wiggles and waggles from one end of his shaggy body to the other.

I motioned for Tilly to sit, which she did immediately. Jagger, who Brady estimated to be about eight months old, plopped his butt on the ground right next to her. I praised them both and told them to stay. I walked away and spoke to Brady for a minute, keeping an eye on the pair as I did. After a minute, I motioned for the dogs to come and then sit and stay again. I asked both Jagger and Tilly to repeat the behavior several times, praising both dogs when my hand gesture was met with an appropriate response. When a dog was in training, repetition was key. Experience had shown that if a behavior was repeated often enough, even easily distractible dogs such as Jagger would begin to respond to the hand flip even when Tilly wasn't around to show him what to do.

Once I'd released them to relax, Jagger came over to say hi. I knelt to greet the terrier and was welcomed with wet, sloppy kisses. The fact that

Jagger now seemed delighted to see me when he'd all but ignored me in those first days was progress in my book.

"Where's Bowie?" I asked about the second terrier.

"In his pen," Brady answered as his blue eyes met my brown. "I've decided the only way I'm going to make any progress training the boys is to separate them for individual sessions. Initially, I tried joint sessions, but that wasn't getting me anywhere. I figure once I have them responding individually, I can bring them together for training for short periods of time." Brady bent over and greeted Tilly, allowing her to enthusiastically rain doggy kisses on his face.

"Seems like you have a good plan. How can I help?"

"I'm glad you asked. I hoped you and Tilly would have time to work with the brothers and me on Saturday. Between the clinic and the shelter, it's hard to make time for the specialized training they need. Besides, Tilly is a good influence on Bowie and Jagger. They seem to settle down and pay more attention when she's with them."

Brady had a point. Tilly was an old pro at responding to both hand and verbal signals. When she was around, Jagger and Bowie tended to mimic whatever she was doing.

"Tilly and I would be happy to help," I answered. "Did you have anything specific in mind?" Brady interviewed prospective doggy parents to find out exactly what they were looking for in a dog. He wanted to ensure that the dogs he placed were perfect matches for their new humans. If the shelter housed a dog who seemed to be compatible overall with one of the humans who came looking for a forever friend, more often than not Brady was willing to provide extra training to ensure the dog met the needs of whoever they'd spend their life with.

"I spoke to Jimmy Early. He came in to adopt one dog, but after we spoke, he said he'd be willing to consider the brothers provided they loved the water, were comfortable on a SUP board, and enjoyed traveling."

I knew Jimmy. He and his girlfriend, Destiny, operated a paddleboat and stand-up paddleboard concession at the lake during the spring and summer. Once the snow began to fall, they packed up their belongings and took off in their camper for warmer climes. It made sense they'd want to adopt dogs who liked the water and travel. "Have you tried the boys in the water?"

Brady nodded. "They aren't fans of the wet stuff. Tilly likes to swim. Maybe we can take the boys to the beach on Saturday and Tilly can show them how much fun it is. Once we get them used to the water, we can work on the SUP board. As for traveling, they seem fine riding around in my truck, so I don't think that will be a problem."

"Okay. I can do Saturday. Say around ten?"

"Ten would be perfect."

I paused to put the appointment in my phone calendar. "The reason I'm here now," I said, once I'd finished the entry, "is because I wanted to pick up some more of that nutrient-dense cat food for the kittens." I had adopted two rescues of my own, an orange-stripped kitten named Tang and a black kitten with long fur named Tinder. As a shelter volunteer, I was able to purchase quality pet food at Brady's cost, so it was only the best that my discount, combined with my adequate-but-far-from-generous salary, could buy for my animals.

"I was about to quit for the day," Brady informed me. "Let me bring Jagger back to his brother and I'll go to the clinic with you. You can grab the food as well as the flyers I had made up for the adoption event later this month."

I followed Brady, who was dressed in faded jeans, running shoes, and a dark blue T-shirt. He dressed in slacks, a dress shirt, and a white lab coat when the clinic was open, but when he spent time at the shelter, he dressed down, which was the look I appreciated the most. "Did you decide on a theme for the event?"

Brady's eyes lit up with enthusiasm. "Speed dating. I've arranged to use the football field at the high school. I'm going to section it off into twelve smaller areas using temporary fencing. Each individual pen will have a dog who's available for adoption. Prospective doggy parents will each be assigned to a pen, where they'll spend three minutes. When the time's up, all the people will rotate in a prearranged pattern until everyone has visited all the pens. Once a prospective doggy parent has their visit with each of the twelve dogs, they'll be able to request up to three dogs to spend additional time with. At the end of the event, prospective parents can fill out an application for the dog of their choice."

"Are you going to allow for second and third choices just in case everyone wants the same dog?" It seemed that at almost every adoption clinic I'd ever worked, there were interested parties fighting over a few dogs, while others remained homeless.

He nodded. "Some prospective parents don't do well with this sort of event, and they're of course welcome to come in during the week to look at the dogs individually, but I've done speed-dating events before, and usually, dogs and humans manage to find one another in the time allotted."

"Sounds like fun. I'll start putting the flyers up tomorrow while I'm doing my route."

"If you need more, just ask and I can run some out to you. I want this event to be a success, and I'm hoping we're starting early enough this time to plaster the entire town."

"I'll make sure every bulletin board and store window in White Eagle has a flyer."

I got the cat food and flyers from Brady's veterinary clinic, and Tilly and I piled into my Jeep and headed home: a small, rustic cabin outside the town limits of White Eagle. While the plumbing was old and the heater temperamental, the view of the mountains from both my front and back decks was truly spectacular. The cabin was surrounded by national forest and my closest neighbor was far enough away that I couldn't see any other buildings from any window.

When I pulled into the private drive that led from the highway to the cabin, I spotted my good friend Tony Marconi sitting in his truck in front of the cabin. Tony and I had met in middle school. He was not only the smartest kid in our entire school, but he was also sort of a geek. I'll admit that when I first met him, I, like the other kids, had made fun of his looks and superior intellect, but after he helped me out with a mystery that resulted in the two of us sharing a pretty huge secret, the tall and gangly genius had grown on me and eventually become one of my very best friends.

Of course, now that he was an adult and had grown into his height, he was not only the smartest man I knew but the sexiest as well. Not that I would *ever* tell him that. We were, after all, just friends.

"What are you doing here?" I asked as I climbed out of the Jeep and Tony kissed me on the cheek. "Not that I'm not thrilled to see you; I just wasn't expecting you."

"I was in town and thought I'd stop by to see if you wanted to have a pizza-and-video-game night. It's been a while."

"It has been a while," I answered as Tilly jumped out of the Jeep and greeted Tony's dog, Titan, with a wagging tail and tiny leaps of joy. "And I don't have plans tonight. I wish I'd known what you had in mind. I would have stopped to pick up the food on my way home."

"No need. I have a pizza warming in your oven and a new microbrew I've been wanting to try in your refrigerator."

After Titan greeted Tilly, he trotted over to say hi to me, while Tilly greeted Tony. "If you had a way into the cabin, why were you waiting out here in your truck?"

"It seemed presumptuous to wait inside. I knew you probably wouldn't be long, it's a beautiful evening, and you do have quite the spectacular view here."

I ruffled Titan behind the ears, then kissed him on the top of the head. "I'm glad you're here, but you probably should have called. What if I wasn't free?"

Tony shrugged as Tilly and Titan headed to my front door together. "I would have taken my beer and pizza home. Let me just grab a few things from my truck and I'll get the game set up."

"Do you have a new one?"

"I do. It's called Valley of Atonement. I've been asked to test it for a friend. You can help."

One of the very best things about Tony, second to his good looks, giving nature, kind heart, millions of dollars, and superior brain, was that he knew a lot of people who developed video games and was always being asked to test them and offer advice before they were on the market. Most of the time he asked me and his other friend, Shaggy, to test them out as well.

"I hope you didn't order pineapple on the pizza," I said as I walked to the door with Tony trailing behind me.

"I would never get pineapple on any pizza I planned to share with you. There are also no mushrooms, peppers, or tomatoes. All meat, all the way."

I grinned. "Thanks. I know you love pineapple on your pizza, so I appreciate the sacrifice. Why don't you set everything up while I change out of my work clothes?" As a mail carrier, I had a uniform I was required to wear every day, but when I was home, it was sweatpants, jeans, or shorts.

I greeted both kittens and headed into my bedroom, where I put on a pair of jeans and a T-shirt. I pulled my long hair into a ponytail, then returned to the main living area of the cabin, where Tony had the pizza on the table, along with plates, forks, and ice-cold beer. It was a beautiful day and I was tempted to move the dinner outdoors onto my deck, but it was still a little chilly in the evenings, although the snow had melted and the meadows were lush with green grass and colorful wildflowers.

"This really is the best pizza in town," I said as I took my first bite of the thickly layered pie.

"Having Giovani's Pizza on a regular basis is one of the things I miss about not living closer to town," Tony said. "I noticed they had a few new specialties, including a buffalo chicken topping that sounds like it might be fun to try."

"That does sound good. We'll have to try it next time." I slipped a second piece of pizza onto my plate. "Shaggy loves chicken wings, so I'm betting he'd like to try it as well." Shaggy owned a video game store, and the two spent quite a bit of time together. "I'm surprised you didn't bring him with you tonight."

"I thought about inviting him, but I wanted to talk to you about something."

I set my slice down. "My dad?"

Tony had been trying to help me track down my father, who supposedly died twelve years ago. For some reason, I had a feeling there was more to his death than I'd been told, so I'd asked Tony to look in to it. Not only had he found what seemed like proof that Dad hadn't died in the fiery accident, as everyone thought, but there was every indication he could still be alive and living an alternate life.

"No, not your dad," Tony said.

"Okay." I couldn't imagine what Tony would want to discuss with me that he wouldn't want Shaggy to overhear if it wasn't regarding my father and his not-so-dead state of being. "Then what is it?"

Tony paused and made eye contact before he continued. Okay, he was making me nervous now. It wasn't like Tony to hesitate. I watched as a myriad of emotions crossed his face. Eventually, he spoke. "Remember you asked me to check out the man who came to White Eagle to visit your mother over Valentine's Day?"

"I remember. His name is Romero Montenegro. He lives in Italy, where his family owns a winery. You said he checked out. You said he used to work in a museum but now teaches history at a university in Rome, although he's been on sabbatical. You said he'd never been married or arrested, though he did have one failed engagement seven years ago. You said he seemed like a good guy. Did you find something else?"

Tony hesitated. Oh, I didn't like the look on his face. Tony was the sort who was always confident and sure. This look of doubt and indecision didn't suit him at all.

"What is it?" I asked in a much firmer tone.

"Is your mom still seeing him?" Tony asked.

"He went back to Italy, so I guess she isn't technically seeing him, but they're still corresponding. She's even made some noises to Ruthie and me about taking some time off over the summer so she can go to Italy to visit him. I've been trying to talk her out of it. I mean, she's fifty-six and the mother of two adults, and he's a forty-two-year-old playboy. I don't see what she sees in the man. They have absolutely nothing in common."

Tony raised an eyebrow. I knew what he wasn't saying. Romero was a total babe in a cover-of-a-romance-novel way. Dark and fit, with a polished air and a wonderful accent. Of course my middle-aged mother would find him attractive. She'd have to be dead not to be. But sizzling-hot sex appeal wasn't everything. Though in Romero's case, it might be enough.

"Do you think we can move on from this line of thought?" I asked. "The idea of my mother having those types of feelings sort of grosses me out."

"I guess I can understand that."

"So, what's the deal? Why are we even discussing the Casanova who's caught my mother's attention?"

Tony splayed his hands on the table, his long fingers open wide. "I'm not sure why I even continued to look into his past after that initial search, but something felt off, so when I had some free time, I poked around a bit more. Remember I told you that Romero hadn't been married but he'd had a failed engagement seven years ago?"

"Yeah. So?"

"It looks like he didn't break up with his fiancée, but she didn't break up with him either."

I sat back in my chair and crossed my arms over my chest. "Okay, what are you saying? Is the guy my mom has been fooling around with still engaged?"

"No. He's not engaged. Romero Montenegro didn't get married because his engagement failed. The reason he didn't get married was because his fiancée died. She was, in fact, murdered."

Chapter 2

"Murdered?" I felt my heart rate quicken. "Please don't tell me that Romero was a suspect."

"Okay, I won't tell you."

I put my hands on the top of my head as if to prevent it from exploding. "God! I can't believe this. My very sweet and conservative mother is having a fling with a cold-blooded killer."

Tony took my hands in his, lifting them down from my head. "At this point we don't know anything for sure. All we know is that the murder is still being actively investigated. Based on what I was able to discover, it does seem Romero is considered a suspect."

"It's been seven years. Why on earth hasn't the murder been solved yet?"

"I don't have all the details. Yet. I'm looking in to it."

"Do you know anything at all yet?"

Tony nodded. "I've uncovered a few facts, which will provide a place to start a more formal investigation. I'm sorry I didn't dig deeper when you first asked me to. If something had happened to your mother, I would never have forgiven myself."

I took a deep breath and blew it out. "It's okay. There was a lot going on when I asked you to run the initial search, and my mom is fine. Besides, you did ask me if I wanted you to dig deeper and I said no. We had other fish to fry. The question now is, what do I do? Do I tell my mom what you found out, even though we don't have much, or do I wait until we have more and can assess the situation?"

"It seems to me that unless Romero comes to town or your mother makes plans to visit him in Italy, maybe we should keep what we know to ourselves until we can find out more about what's going on."

I nodded. "Yeah. That's a good idea. What's your next step?"

"Just to start digging and follow whatever leads I stumble upon." Tony picked up Tinder, who'd jumped into his lap, and set him gently on the floor. "Should we tell Mike?"

Mike was my brother, who also happened to be a cop.

"No. He's so protective of Mom. He'll probably go ballistic when he finds out she has a friend of the romantic variety in the first place. It would be better to wait until we know more."

"Okay. That makes sense."

Suddenly, it felt like the walls of my little cabin were closing in on me. I hadn't been comfortable with my mother's relationship with Romero from the beginning, and now I wished he'd just go away. The relationship never had made sense. Not only was Romero younger than my mom, but they lived so far apart. I didn't see Mom moving away from Mike and me, and I doubted Romero would move away from his country, culture, and family, so what was the point of the friendship in the first place? "How about we take a walk after we finish eating? It's a little chilly, but we still have at least an hour of sunlight. We can burn off all the calories we just consumed, and maybe you can catch me up on everything you already know."

"I'm done eating if you are."

I nodded.

"Grab a jacket while I put the rest of the pizza in your refrigerator."

I did as Tony suggested and grabbed what I referred to as my spring jacket, which wasn't as heavy as my winter parka. Tony said he had a jacket in his truck, which he'd get on his way out. I found two leashes even though we most likely wouldn't need them and went toward the front door.

We walked maybe a quarter of a mile along the narrow dirt trail without speaking. Titan and Tilly ran ahead, stopping to sniff every log and interesting shrub they came across. The woods around my cabin must have all sorts of wonderful smells, especially now that the spring flowers were beginning to bloom. Titan became overly interested in a nurse log to the point that he seemed to forget all about us. After a moment, Tony called him over so we could keep both dogs in our line of sight.

Eventually, when I felt ready, I turned to Tony. "Why don't you tell me everything you've learned and we can work together from this point forward?"

"Keep in mind, what I have are random pieces of information that may not mean anything. I think it's important we keep an open mind until we know more."

"Okay," I agreed as we started walking again, meandering through the forest until we reached the river, flowing rapidly with the season's runoff. We'd need to keep an eye on the dogs and call them back if they got too close. During the late summer and fall, the river was shallow enough to wade through from one side to the other, but the runoff provided a significant danger to anyone or anything that dared venture into it. "Start at the beginning, and don't leave anything out."

"When I did the initial search into his background, I didn't find any evidence of a marriage for Romero, though there was mention of him having been engaged to Luciana Parisi, who lived in the same region of Italy he did. I assumed the pair had ended things and didn't think anything of it; her name didn't mean anything to me and broken engagements are common. We were busy with something else and I didn't see the point in digging deeper. Once things slowed down a bit, I did some additional research and found Luciana was the great-great-granddaughter of Ferraro Parisi, who at one time was best friends with Romero's great-great-grandfather, Damico Montenegro. I later learned that while Ferraro and Damico started out as friends, they died as enemies."

"Enemies? Why?"

"It seems both started wineries at about the same time, and both did well. In fact, they quickly escalated in status in the region, and the men spent their careers trading number-one and -two rankings, which seemed to create an urgency between them to gain a foothold over the other."

"Am I picking up on some sort of Capulets versus Montagues sort of thing?"

Tony nodded. "In a way. The men became sworn enemies and a family feud was born that lasted for almost a century, until Romero and Luciana decided to put an end to it and became friends. Their friendship seemed to have begun when they were in high school and continued into adulthood. As far as I can tell, they began to date when Romero was in his early thirties. They became engaged eight years ago and Luciana died a year later."

"Wow. That's really sad." I ventured toward a path that led away from the river. The dogs were well trained and had stayed away from the powerful water, but I felt better putting some distance between us and the potential for tragedy. "Why was Romero considered a suspect?"

"Initially, Luciana's father accused Romero of using his daughter to obtain the secret blend of grapes that helped him win a regional competition five years in a row. He asserted Romero not only seduced his daughter into giving away family secrets but, once he had them, had no more use for her, so he killed her. Romero denied having anything to do with Luciana's death, but he was unable to provide an alibi. He told the investigator he was at a retreat on the weekend Luciana died."

We paused to choose a route around a dead tree that had fallen across the trail. "Sounds like a pretty good alibi to me."

"It would have been, but he couldn't prove he was where he said he was. It seems he'd been sworn to secrecy regarding the whereabouts of the retreat, as well as the identity of the other members of the club who attended it."

I frowned. "Why all the secrecy?"

Tony shrugged as he stepped over the fallen branches, which allowed us to continue down the path. "While historically there have been secret societies with political influence in Italy, such as the Freemasons and the Carbonari, given Romero's connection to both the museum and university, I suspect the group he belongs to is made up of academics, although that's just a guess."

I raised a brow. "I was a member of a secret club with some friends when I was a kid. It certainly made us feel special. But adults?"

"It does seem sort of silly, although I have no idea the nature of this group. The thing that's important to our discussion is that Romero's attendance at this retreat greatly influenced his inability to provide a better alibi. Because he couldn't prove where he was when Luciana was murdered, the local law enforcement had no choice but to look at him as a potential suspect."

"But he was cleared?"

"Eventually, a man named Angelo Longorian confessed to killing Luciana. He told the investigator assigned to the case it had been an accident and he'd never meant to hurt her. Apparently, they were both drunk, and they argued. She came at him with a statue she grabbed from a nearby table, threatening to hit him with it, he pushed her, and she fell and hit her head. The evidence at the scene of the murder supported the story Longorian told, so there was no reason to doubt him. He was convicted of manslaughter, but given his status in local society, he served very little prison time."

Once the trail was free of debris, Tony accepted a stick Titan brought him. He tossed it farther up the trail, and both dogs took off after it.

"So, what happened to change the investigator's opinion that Longorian had accidentally killed Luciana?"

"He was killed in an auto accident. Initially, the accident was considered just that—a tragic yet random event—but after looking into things, it was determined that the vehicle Longorian was driving had been run off the road. During the investigation into his death, they found that Longorian had spent a lot of time in the United States and had, in fact, been here, not in Italy, on the weekend Luciana died."

Oh, I didn't like the way this was beginning to sound. "Longorian lied. Why? Why would anyone confess to a murder they didn't commit?"

Titan returned with the stick. He dropped it at Tony's feet. Tony threw it again. Titan loved to play fetch, and once he got the game started, he was unlikely to quit until Tony put an end to it. "I don't know for certain, but I found out that shortly after Longorian confessed to contributing to Luciana's death, he suddenly had a lot of money to burn, despite the fact that he'd previously been struggling financially. The investigator was unable to trace the source of the money, and now that Longorian is dead, he can't ask him about the sudden influx of funds. The two events—the confession and the change in finances—might have been unrelated, but then again…"

"But if it walks like a duck and talks like a duck..." I looked directly at Tony. The sun had begun its descent behind the mountain and the low rays of sunlight reflected off his dark hair. "Does it seem odd that the investigator didn't bother to check on Longorian's whereabouts when he confessed?"

"In retrospect, not digging further turned out to be a considerable oversight, but this was a high-profile murder with no solid leads, so a confession must have seemed like a blessing. Besides, the investigator most likely had no reason to suspect Longorian would confess to a murder he didn't commit even if it was an accident."

Tony had a point. The investigator probably had no reason to doubt Longorian, especially if he had no other suspects. "So what does all this mean? Do you think Romero is guilty of killing Luciana, because frankly, it's beginning to sound that way to me."

"I wouldn't say I necessarily believe Romero is guilty of murder simply because he might have known the truth and lied," Tony countered. "It does, however, cause me concern."

"Okay, so what now?" I asked. "We know Longorian was out of the country, so someone else killed Luciana. It may still have been an accident, but that seems irrelevant when the guilty party let an innocent man go to prison. If we can't prove or disprove Romero's alibi, how do we find out whether he's guilty?"

Tony took my hand in his and turned to head down a path that looped back to the cabin. "I've given that some thought. I have a friend who works with Interpol, so he has contacts in law enforcement around the world. I'll contact him to see if he knows anything. It might take a while for him to get back to me, but there's no urgency as long as your mom stays here and Romero stays there. And I'll keep poking around to see what I can find. I'm not saying I'll be able to figure this out given the limited information I have to work with, but maybe something will pop up."

"And maybe the friendship my mom has established with him will fade now that he's gone back to Italy."

"Maybe."

Tony and I walked in silence for several minutes. I so enjoyed spending time at the end of the day walking through the silent forest with him, Tilly, and Titan. The simple activity somehow made me feel centered in a world that at times seemed chaotic. "As you know, I haven't been happy about my mom's relationship with Romero, though it's shown me something important."

"And what's that?"

"I can see she's ready to move on with her life. My dad has been gone for twelve years, and as far as I know, before Romero showed up, she hadn't gone on a single date. At first, I wasn't sure I was ready to see her dating, but now, I realize she's been lonely. She deserves to have someone to share her life with. Someone to come home to at the end of the day." I reached down and ruffled Tilly behind the ears. I thanked God every day I had Tilly, Tang, and Tinder to come home to. "She needs someone who's here, though, in White Eagle. Someone who can be a real partner to her. Not some playboy living so far away."

Tony didn't say anything, though he put his arm around my shoulders and gave them a squeeze. I laid my head on his shoulder. I was lucky to have someone in my life who was always there for me. Someone I could count on, no matter the situation.

Back at the cabin, I stomped the dirt from my feet before opening the front door and motioning Tony and the dogs inside. I filled the dogs' water dishes, then slipped off my shoes and kicked them into a corner. The sun had set and the sky was beginning to darken, so I clicked on a couple of lamps. I checked my answering machine, then grabbed a couple of bottles from the refrigerator.

"So, how about that game of Atonement?" Tony asked as I handed him a beer.

I glanced at the game. "It seems late to just be getting started."

"Okay, then how about we build a fire in your pit, sit on the deck, and drink our beer tonight. We can play the game tomorrow night at my place. I'll even make you dinner."

I nodded. "Okay. I'll bring the kittens and an overnight bag in case it gets late and I decide to stay over."

Tony grinned. "Been a while since we had a slumber party."

"Been a while since you had a video game to test. Should you invite Shaggy?"

Tony's smile faded just a bit. "If you want. I'll call him in the morning to see if he's available. For now, let's get that fire started. Been a while since we sat on the deck and watched the world grow dark."

Chapter 3

Friday, May 4

Tilly and I headed into town the next morning to cover our last route of the week. It was only a little over a week until Mother's Day, and the influx of mail created by colorful cards was beginning to make its way into the daily delivery. So far, we'd gotten away with a single mail bag a day, but my bet was that by next Monday it would be another thing entirely.

"Oh good, you're here." My best friend, Bree Price, met me at the door of her bookstore, the Book Boutique, when I arrived with the day's mail. "I tried calling you at home last night, but you didn't answer."

"I was sitting on the deck with Tony. I guess I didn't hear it ring. So, what's up? Why were you trying to get hold of me?"

Bree handed me a card in a pink envelope. "I'm not sure what to do with this."

"It's a card. I guess you should open it."

Bree rolled her eyes. "I did open it. I opened it last night when I opened all the mail you dropped off yesterday. I didn't realize until after I did that it wasn't for me."

"Ah, this got mixed in with your mail and you want me to get it to the rightful recipient?"

"There's more to it than that. Look at the address on the envelope."

The address was correct, but the name wasn't Bree Price or the Book Boutique, but rather Edna Fairchild of Edna's Antiques.

"Edna Fairchild used to own the antique store in this building four or five years ago," I commented as it dawned on me how the error had been made.

"I know that," Bree said. "It's obvious whoever sent the card wasn't aware that she'd closed her store. Normally, I'd simply ask that you deliver it to her home, but ..."

"Edna passed away," I finished for Bree.

"Exactly. My first thought was to send the card back to the sender with a message, but there's no return address. The postmark is Chicago, but I'm not sure that will do us any good without a name."

"I can send it over to the dead letter department. In cases like this, there's only so much we can do."

Bree frowned, her perfectly shaped brows narrowing above her bright blue eyes. "Read the card."

I set down my bag and opened it. On the left inner flap was the following message:

Hi Mom,

I bet you weren't expecting to hear from me, but as Mother's Day approaches, and I think of the good times we once shared, my resolve never to speak to you again for what went down almost a quarter of a century ago has wavered. I've spent some time thinking about everything that happened, and I think I'm finally ready to admit that at least part of the blame for our estrangement falls directly on my shoulders. Life is too short to hang on to grudges from the past, and I want to put this behind us so we can enjoy the years we have left. I know the depth of the pain we inflicted on each other runs deep, but if you're willing to put it behind you and give us another chance, I'm ready to apologize for my part in our estrangement and forgive you for your part. If you can find it in your heart to give us a second chance, meet me in our special place at noon on Mother's Day.

Sincerely,
The Prodigal Child

I looked at Bree. "Wow. I guess whoever sent this has no idea their mother has passed."

Bree tucked a lock of her long blond hair behind one ear. "I feel like we should track down this person and let them know Edna died six months ago. I'm just not sure how to do it."

In all the time I'd known Edna, she'd lived alone in a small house just one block over from Main

Street. She'd spent most of her time at the antique store until a stroke forced her to slow down. She'd continued to live on her own for a few more years after closing the store, but eventually, she'd been forced to move to an assisted-living facility in Kalispell. I seemed to remember reading she'd passed away just before the holidays.

"We're too young to remember her child if he or she left twenty-five years ago, but my mom or Aunt Ruthie might. I still need to drop off the mail at the café, so I'll ask them. If they don't remember, Tilly and I will go back by to talk to Hap or Hattie. If Edna's child ever lived here, I'm sure someone will remember them. Once we have a name, I'll have Tony do a search for a phone number or address. I'll call you later to let you know what I find out."

"Thanks, Tess. I knew you'd be able to help. Do you want to grab dinner tonight?"

I picked up my mailbag and slung it over my shoulder. "I have plans with Tony tonight. Maybe next week."

Bree raised one brow. "Tony? Didn't you just say you were hanging out with Tony last night?"

"I did."

"Is there something going on I should know about?"

"Nothing's going on. Tony has a new video game to test. I'd invite you to come along, but I think Tony plans to ask Shaggy, and I know the two of you don't get along."

Bree crossed her arms over her breezy yellow blouse. "That's an understatement. I guess I'll just stay in tonight and do laundry."

"At least you won't have to deal with it on Saturday." I glanced at the clock. "I need to go if I'm going to have time to check with everyone about Edna's child. I'll call you later."

Tilly and I had made good time that afternoon, so I figured I'd have extra time to spend on the mystery of the Mother's Day card. The café was busy when I arrived, so I slipped into a booth, motioned for Tilly to slide under the table, then let my mom know I needed to speak to her when she had a few minutes. She delivered food to a table before sitting down across from me.

"What's up?" she asked, brushing away a strand of hair that had worked its way loose from her serviceable bun.

"Bree received a Mother's Day card that was meant for Edna Fairchild. The envelope doesn't have a return address, but based on the contents of the card, it appears it was sent to her by her child. I hoped you'd remember the name so we can track him or her down."

Mom furrowed her brow. "Edna did have a son. He must have been around twenty when he left White Eagle. I seemed to remember them having a falling out. I never saw him again after he left, and Edna stopped talking about him altogether. It was creepy in a way. It was as if she completely cut him out of her life. She acted like she'd never even had a son."

"Do you remember his name?"

Mom pursed her lips as she appeared to be considering my question. "I was a young wife and mother back then and didn't have money to spend on antiques, so I didn't spend any time in her store. I barely knew Edna until much later, but I think her son

35

was named Craig, or maybe it was Carl. I didn't know him, but I seem to remember he was a wild one. You know, it might have been Curt." Mom's eyes narrowed as she focused on the name. Her eyes grew big. "Or maybe it was Clint, or possibly Cliff. You might ask Hattie. She didn't own the bakeshop back then, but she also didn't have children to tend to, so she had a lot more free time than most. She liked to socialize with the merchants on Main."

"I'll head over there next."

"Dinner on Sunday?" Mom asked.

I knew it was important to my mom that Mike and I come to Sunday dinner as often as possible, but I didn't want to be put in the position of making small talk with her until I knew more about Romero's role in the death of his fiancée. I wasn't very good at covering my thoughts and I was afraid my expression would give me away if his name came up in conversation. "I have plans this Sunday, but I'm totally on for Mother's Day. And you aren't going to cook. You and Mike can come to my place. He can barbecue some ribs and I'll make the sides and a dessert."

Mom hesitated for just a minute and then smiled. "It is beautiful out at your place at this time of year. Maybe we can eat outdoors if it's warm."

"That's a wonderful idea. Is Aunt Ruthie going to Johnny's?"

Mom nodded.

"Okay, then it'll just be the three of us."

"Bree is probably going to spend time with her own mother, but you should invite Brady," Mom suggested. "He doesn't have family in town, and he and Mike get along well."

It looked like Mom was on duty as a matchmaker even on Mother's Day. "I think Brady has plans, but if you don't mind, I might ask Tony. He probably won't be busy."

A thoughtful look crossed Mom's face. "You've been spending a lot of time with him lately."

I shrugged. "We're friends. Have been for a very long time."

"Yes, I guess you have. I think it would be lovely to invite Tony. It's been a while since you've brought him around. It'll be nice to catch up."

"Okay, I'll ask him. I'll ask Bree too, just in case she doesn't have plans with her mom. I sort of remember her mother was going to spend the weekend at Bree's sister's in Fargo."

I left the café and headed down the block to Grandma Hattie's Bakeshop. The first thing I noticed upon entering, the first thing I *always* notice when visiting Hattie's bakery, is the smell. It's like entering a corner of heaven. It was only an hour until closing and most of the doughnuts, muffins, and cookies, had already been sold, but there was something in the oven that was sending my senses into overdrive.

"What is that heavenly smell?" I asked after nodding to Hattie's dog, Bruiser. Bruiser didn't like to be touched by anyone other than her, so I didn't touch, but I'd noticed he seemed to be fine with a casual acknowledgment of his presence.

"Cinnamon pecan cake for my women's group," Hattie answered after handing Tilly one of the small dog cookies she always had on hand.

"Sounds wonderful. I don't suppose you made an extra cake to sell?"

"Sorry. I do still have a lovely blueberry cake with crumb topping that's been doing well today, though. Add a dollop of whipped cream to the top and you have a real treat."

"I'll take it with me. I'm having dinner with Tony tonight and he loves blueberries."

Hattie smiled and began boxing the cake.

"I came back to ask you about Edna Fairchild." I explained about the card Bree had received by accident. "I hoped you'd remember the son."

"I remember him. That boy broke his mama's heart."

"I gathered that by the note he wrote. It seems he's ready to make amends, although it's too late for that. Still, we'd like to get hold of him to let him know his mama passed. Do you happen to remember his name?"

"Everyone called him Chip, but I'm not sure that was his real name."

"Do you have any idea how to get hold of him?"

Hattie shook her head. "I'm sorry. I have no idea where he went when he left White Eagle. Edna never spoke of him again. I think it was just too painful for her, so she went on with her life like she'd never had a kid in the first place."

"Did Chip have any friends he might have stayed in touch with? Maybe someone who's still around and might be able to provide his contact information?"

"I seem to remember him being friends with Rupert Hanson. I guess if anyone might know what had become of Chip, it would be him."

Rupert was a contractor who still lived in the area. I didn't know him well, but he knew Mike, and I'd met him a time or two, so if I called him to ask about

Chip, he might be willing to talk to me. I thanked Hattie for the information, paid for my cake, and took Tilly back to my Jeep. I needed to drop off my mailbag before I headed out to Tony's, but I decided to talk to Mike about Rupert first, because I had to walk right by his office on my way back to the beginning of my route. When I entered the small police station, I was greeted by Frank Hudson, Mike's partner.

"Is Mike in?" I asked after returning his greeting.

"In his office. I'd tread lightly. He seems to be in a foul mood."

"He's been in a foul mood a lot lately," I observed. "He hasn't mentioned that anything's wrong, has he?"

Frank shook his head. "You know Mike. He's not one to share. Based on some of the comments he's made, however, I think his problem may have to do with a girl, or in his case, the lack of one."

I frowned. "Mike's a personable, popular guy. He's never had a problem getting female attention when he wants it."

Frank shrugged. "I don't disagree. If his problem isn't female-related, I have no idea what's up. He's your brother. Maybe he'll talk to you."

I laughed. "Unlikely. Mike has never confided in me. I see no reason for him to start now. Listen, you don't have a phone number for Rupert Hanson, do you?" It suddenly occurred to me that if Mike was in one of his moods, it might be best to avoid him altogether.

"Sorry. He might be listed in the book, although there are fewer folks with landlines these days."

"Yeah. I guess I'll have to risk Mike's cranky mood to ask him. Is it okay if Tilly waits here with you?"

"Fine by me."

I walked down the narrow hallway to Mike's office. The door was open, but he didn't seem to be paying attention to his surroundings, so I knocked anyway.

"Tess." Mike looked surprised to find me standing at his door. "What are you doing here?"

"I wondered if you had a phone number for Rupert Hanson."

Mike sat back and crossed his arms over his broad chest. "Yeah, I have it. Why do you need it?"

I briefly explained about the card Bree had received and our desire to notify Chip about his mother's death.

"I'll call Rupert for you," Mike offered. "See if he has contact information for Chip. If he does, I'll call Chip and notify him of his mother's passing. Notifying next of kin sort of comes with the job description. If Rupert doesn't have a way to get in touch with Chip, I'll do some digging around on my end. I'll call you either way. Will you be home tonight?"

"I'll be at Tony's, but you can call my cell. If I don't answer, it'll be because we're in the basement. There isn't any cell reception down there. Just leave a message and I'll call you back."

"Okay. How's Tony doing anyway? It's been a while since I've run into him."

I leaned a hip against the doorframe. "He's good. Been busy. I hadn't seen him for quite a while myself, but he showed up at my place last night and asked if I wanted to help him test a video game. Seemed like fun, so I agreed. Ended up taking a walk instead, so I'm going over to his place for a rain check tonight. Do you have any plans for your Friday night?"

Mike scowled. "Not a one."

I supposed after what Frank had said, I probably shouldn't have asked that question, but it had slipped out. "You should call Bree," I suggested. "She wanted to have dinner tonight, but I already had plans with Tony. She might be happy for an alternate to grab a bite with."

Mike gave a little half smile. "You don't think she's made other plans by now?"

I shrugged. "You won't know for sure until you ask, but I spoke to her less than an hour ago, so I sort of doubt it. Call her. If she's busy, you're no worse off than you are now, and if she isn't busy, you'll have someone to grab a meal with."

"Okay. I just might do that."

Chapter 4

Tony lived on a large, isolated estate about halfway up the mountain, which put him a good twenty minutes from town. His amazing home was located on a private lake he skated on in the winter and fished in the summer. When he first bought the property and built the huge house, I thought living alone so far from his friends might get lonely. But when I realized how busy Tony was, working on all the projects he appeared to make millions from, and observed his contracting schedule up close, I understood why he probably enjoyed the solitude, which allowed him more time to focus on his work.

The house had a huge living area, most of which was dog and cat friendly. The clean room, which housed his computers and other specialty equipment, was in a finished and insolated basement. Due to the sensitive nature of the equipment, the animals weren't allowed there, but they didn't seem to mind because Tony made sure to have comfy beds and lots of toys in pretty much every other room. I'd begun spending nights over at Tony's from time to time after we began to research my dad's disappearance, and somewhere along the way, one of the guest rooms had been officially designated as "Tess's room."

I put my bag there and then headed back into the living area, where Tony was greeting Tilly and the cats. "I hope you're hungry. I made a pot of my chili."

"I'm starving," I said as my stomach began to rumble. "It's warm this evening. Why don't we eat on the deck overlooking the water?"

"You read my mind. I already wiped everything down, so all we need to do is grab the food and utensils. Maybe we can take a walk around the lake after we eat. It'll give the dogs a chance to tire themselves out before we settle in with the game."

I grabbed spoons and napkins while Tony scooped the chili into brown stoneware bowls. He'd made corn bread to go with the chili, so I brought out small plates as well as butter and knives. Tony chose to have a beer, so I had one as well. Once everything was set up out on the table overlooking the water, we settled in to enjoy Tony's special recipe. I wasn't sure what he did to make his chili so tasty, but it was the best I'd ever had. I'd asked him for his recipe, but he'd told me it was a family secret that could only be handed down to relatives; if I wanted it, I'd have to marry him. Marriage seemed like a big step to take just for a chili recipe, though every time I ate a bowl of the spicy yet flavorful meal from Nirvana, I found myself wanting to agree to do just that.

"Is Shaggy coming by?" I asked after I'd eaten almost half a bowl of yummy goodness.

"He had plans to bowl with some of the guys who live in his apartment building, so it's just you and me."

"Just as well. I want all the credit and glory when I take you down and make you beg for mercy."

Tony choked on his corn bread. "Beg for mercy?"

I grinned. "You know what I mean. I realize I sometimes take it easy on you, but tonight I'm out for the sweet joy of victory."

Tony chuckled. "Okay. Fairly warned."

We both knew the only way I ever beat him at anything was if he let me win, which wasn't often, but the pre-event banter was part of the fun, so I gave it my best, even if I didn't have a chance of winning the sure-to-be-complex and fast-paced game.

"Before I forget, I wanted to invite you to my place for a barbecue on Mother's Day if you don't have plans."

Tony looked surprised by my invite. "Won't you be spending the day with your mother?"

"She'll be there. Mike too. She suggested I invite Brady because he's new in town, but I know he's busy, and it occurred to me that you probably wouldn't have plans. Mom's always been fond of you. She said it would be good to catch up."

"Are you sure?" Tony looked uncertain. "It seems sort of like a day you'd want to spend with family."

"I'm sure, and you *are* family. So how about it?"

Tony shrugged. "Okay, if you're sure your mom and brother are both fine with it."

"They are. Come after church. Maybe around one-thirty. I hope the weather cooperates. It snowed on Mother's Day a few years ago and we ended cooking the ribs in the oven and eating in the kitchen."

After dinner, I helped Tony with the dishes and then we headed out for our walk. Tilly and Titan were thrilled as they chased squirrels and splashed around in the water, and I was happy and relaxed from the warm weather and excellent company. Tony and I chatted about nothing and everything as we made our way around the lake. He told me about the plans he had for the property, now that the snow had melted, and I shared that I'd been thinking about doing some remodeling on my little cabin. It had been old when I'd bought it and I hadn't done much to it since, so it could use a face-lift.

We were rounding the far end of the lake when my cell rang. "It's my brother," I said. "I should answer."

Tony just nodded.

I hit the Answer button and said hello.

"I talked to Rupert," Mike informed me. "He said Chip was the only name he ever used; if he had a legal name, he didn't know what it was, although if you ask me, I think he was lying."

"Why would he lie?"

"I have no idea, and I don't know for certain he was. It was more of a vibe I picked up. Anyway, Rupert said he hadn't heard from Chip since he left town. He seemed to indicate Chip had reasons to want to disappear, but he wouldn't say what those might be. I asked if he knew of anyone who might have Chip's contact information and he said he didn't."

"That doesn't help much."

"Like I said, I had the feeling Rupert knew more he wasn't telling me, but I didn't have any reason to push him for details. I might call him again on Monday, as sort of a follow-up. That'll give him time to think things over. I got the feeling he knew something that happened in the past. Something significant. Maybe he even knows what caused the rift between Chip and his mother. Like I said, though, if Rupert's protecting some long-held secret, it's up to him to share it or not."

"It'll be hard to find the guy if the only people who know where he might be aren't straight with us."

"I'll put out some feelers tomorrow. I called Bree, as you suggested, and we're going to dinner tonight, so I don't have time to do it now."

"Okay. If nothing else, we can see if there's a male of about the right age living in Chicago with the last name Fairchild."

"It wouldn't hurt to check it out. Listen, I gotta go if I'm going to have time to change out of my uniform before I pick up Bree."

"Have a nice dinner and I'll talk to you tomorrow." I hung up.

Tony looked at me with an expression of interest on his face. I explained about the card Bree had received and our desire to track down Edna's son.

"If you'd like me to look around, we can go down to the computer room when we get back to the house."

"I don't have a lot to go on."

Tony shrugged. "It seems we rarely do. Did Chip grow up here in White Eagle?"

I nodded. "I don't think he was born here, but I'm pretty sure he went to high school here."

"If that's true, there's probably a legal name and photo in the yearbook. If not, he must have had a driver's license. As long as we have some dates to work with, we should be able to find something."

I took Tony's hand in mine and began to walk. "Thanks, Tony. You're a good friend. I probably should have asked you in the first place, but I was sure one of the old-timers would have the information I needed."

"If we don't find what we need tonight, I can set up some programs to work in the background. It might take until tomorrow or even the next day to get a hit, but it's a good starting point. Did I hear you say you were going to the lake with Brady tomorrow?"

"Dog training. We're working on water skills with Bowie and Jagger. I'm meeting him at ten. I should be back by noonish. If it's okay with you, I might just leave Tang and Tinder here. That way I can come back when I finish with Brady and we can work on whatever case we might have new information on. Except for the training, I'm free the rest of the weekend."

Tony squeezed my hand. "Sounds like a good plan. I have a couple of programs working on the Luciana Parisi murder, so we might have some follow-up to do with that."

When we returned to the house we fed the animals and got them settled in their beds in front of the large flat-screen television. We'd only be downstairs for a little while and they never seemed to mind staying behind as long as we turned on Animal Planet or some other pet-friendly show. I wasn't sure if it was the colors or the noises they enjoyed, but all four pets seemed to be watching the story play out on the monitor in front of them when we left the room.

In the basement, Tony sat down at one of the terminals of his huge computer system and I sat down on a chair near him. There was a hum in the background as banks of hard drives with flashing lights worked on programs he'd left running. I knew a lot of the work he did involved decoding files and hacking into secure databases, which meant that while Tony seemed to keep long but reasonable hours, the computers were never at rest.

He keyboarded some commands, and the screen in front of him came to life, displaying a series of folders, each neatly labeled. He created and opened a new folder, then logged onto a program and began typing in search parameters.

"It looks like the high school digitized their yearbooks, which will help. What did you say Chip's last name was?"

"Fairchild."

Tony typed in some commands. "No one by the name of Fairchild. I'll look for someone named Chip." After a moment, a photo of a group of people standing at the end of the football field came up. The names of the individuals were listed, and the last boy on the left was identified as Chip Townsend. "Chip isn't a common name, or even nickname these days, so I'm going to assume this is our Chip. Maybe his mother was divorced from his father, which would account for the differing surnames."

"Okay, that makes sense. Assuming Chip Townsend is our guy, how can we find him?"

Tony typed in a set of commands. "First, I'm searching the yearbook for additional instances of the name Chip Townsend. If that doesn't provide us with anything useful, I'll search the entire high school database. We'll widen the search from there. We can search the local newspaper archives as well as other public records. We'll just keep broadening the net until we hit something. In the meantime, I'll print this photo. Maybe someone in it still lives in town and knows what became of Chip."

I pointed to the screen. "That's Rupert Hanson. Mike already spoke to him and he said he didn't know anything." I moved my finger to a girl with long dark hair standing next to Rupert. "And that's Sue Wade. She looks so different now."

Tony glanced at the photo. "She's older, of course, and she's lightened her hair, but the basic facial structure is the same. There are eight teens in this photo and it appears they're friends. In addition to whatever we can find online, we can speak to whoever's still in White Eagle."

Tony turned back to the keyboard, and I watched in fascination as he worked. His long fingers, which were covered in dark hair, caressed the keyboard in an almost sensual fashion. He certainly could type fast, but it wasn't just that. Tony seemed totally in charge when he was at a computer, demanding that it surrender exactly what he was looking for with every stroke.

"Chip Townsend is listed as a senior in the group photo, but he doesn't have a senior photo and he isn't listed on the page of graduates."

"Do you think he dropped out or was kicked out?"

"Maybe." Tony continued to work. "I'm not finding any additional entries in the yearbook. I'm going to check school records."

I sat forward as images flashed across the screen so quickly, I couldn't tell what Tony was pulling up and then discarding. I had faith he knew what he was looking for and figured he'd know it if he saw it.

"Chip Townsend's legal first name is Greg. He entered White Eagle High School as a sophomore and left in January of his senior year. He was expelled for bringing a gun to school and threatening another student he'd been having problems with."

"You said *threatened* another student. I take it he didn't actually shoot anyone."

Tony shook his head. "All the school record says is that he threatened the student. It doesn't say much of anything else, but I'm betting there was a corresponding police report. Hang on and I'll look."

I knew hacking into the database for the local police department would take longer than it had taken to get into the school's records, so I got up and began to pace around the basement. In times of stress, I found pacing relaxed me. What I didn't understand was why I was stressed in the first place. Chip wasn't someone I knew personally, nor was he anyone who still lived in the area. I'd decided to try to find him so I could have Mike break the news of his mother's death to him, but I didn't have a vested interest in this one way or another. So why the nerves?

"I'm in," Tony said. He worked for a few more minutes, then frowned.

"Problem?"

"The incident occurred when Chip was a minor, so the records have been sealed. He does have an adult record that appears to have been established on his eighteenth birthday. He was arrested for knocking a man unconscious in a bar fight. Over the course of the next two years, there are maybe a dozen other arrests, all minor. Shoplifting, fighting, public intoxication, failing to provide ID to an officer when it was requested. Stuff like that."

"And then?"

"And then nothing. I guess that's when he left town."

I sat back down on my chair. "From what I understand, Chip was about twenty when he left. Is there any indication where he went next?"

"No. I'm going to do a general search using both the names Chip and Greg Townsend. It'll take a few minutes. If nothing comes up right away, I'll have the computer continue to search while we go upstairs and start the game. We can check back every hour or so. If we find what we're looking for, we can take a break from the game."

"And let's not forget the blueberry cake."

Tony smacked his lips. "I've been thinking of that since you brought it in."

Nothing popped after fifteen minutes of looking, so Tony set the search engine up to run and we went upstairs. The two dogs and two cats were curled up on their beds as they were when we'd left them, but they all got up when we entered the room. Tony took the dogs out for a bathroom break while I went into the kitchen, sliced the cake, and opened a bottle of wine. If we were going to settle in and relax, I might as well partake of some of Tony's expensive vino. I picked up the bottle and looked at it. It might very well represent generations of tilling the soil, growing the grapes, perfecting the aging process, and developing new blends, but to me it was simply a beverage to be enjoyed. I knew Tony bought only the very finest wines, so chances were this came from a family vineyard with a long tradition and legacy. I could appreciate that as much as the next person, but then I thought of Romero and wondered if it was worth killing for.

Chapter 5

Saturday, May 5

Tony and I played Atonement until after two in the morning, yet neither of us managed to beat either the game or the other, so we decided to pick up where we'd left off the next evening. Tony's program hadn't had any luck locating Chip or even finding a clue as to where he might have been for the past twenty-five years, but he promised to work on it today, so maybe he'd have news by the time I returned to the house after the training session.

When Tilly and I arrived at the lake, Brady was already there with Jagger and Bowie. He released them just before I opened the Jeep door to let Tilly out. We'd decided to work on the far-eastern side of the lake today because it was less popular with sunbathers, thus less crowded in general. It was an exceptionally warm day, so I'd worn shorts, as had Brady.

The puppies greeted Tilly with wagging tails, delighted yips, and excited jumping, and then Brady and I walked with all three dogs to the place he'd selected for our swimming lesson. Tilly loved the water, so the minute I pulled out the ball I'd brought and tossed it into the lake, she went after it, swimming like a pro as soon as her paws could no longer reach the sand. Bowie and Jagger ran to the edge of the sand and began barking like crazy, but neither entered the water.

Tilly dropped the ball at my feet and I praised her lavishly and offered her a small treat. Then I tossed the ball again, this time instructing Tilly to stay so the boys could have a chance to play. The ball landed at just the edge of the water and both Jagger and Bowie went for it. Bowie was the successful brother this time around, and I offered him praise and a treat. I repeated the behavior, tossing the ball just a bit farther into the water each time. The brothers would go so far as to get their feet wet, but the minute the water touched their underbellies they stopped cold.

I released Tilly from her stay and instructed her to heel. We walked toward the water with Jagger and Bowie nipping at our heels. We reached the water and walked in until we were about knee deep. I offered Tilly a treat, then began an energetic game of tug-of-war with the rope I'd brought along.

Out of the corner of my eye I could see the brothers wanted to join in on the fun. Brady entered the water and we both began to play with Tilly. Jagger, who seemed to be the braver of the two, threw caution to the wind and joined us. After a good ten minutes of play, Bowie finally overcame his reluctance and slowly waded in as well.

Not wanting to push the boys too far too fast, Brady and I worked on entering and exiting the water, not venturing any farther than the boys could easily stand with their heads clear of it. After a lot of play, tons of reinforcement, and an overall good time, I felt they might be ready for the swimming portion of their training on our next visit.

"I want to get them back to the lake right away," Brady said. "Unfortunately, I have a friend coming into town tomorrow, so I'm tied up all day. Would you mind meeting me here on Monday when you get off work? Say six o'clock? I'll even bring food. We can have a picnic."

I used the towel I'd brought to dry my legs and then began drying Tilly. "Monday will work. I think it's supposed to be warm and sunny all week. They did really well today. I think they'll both learn to love the water once they get over their fear."

Brady tossed a couple of balls down the beach and the dogs took off after them. It did my heart good to see the brothers playing and interacting with Tilly and me.

"How's the training going now that you've started with the individual sessions?"

"Much better," Brady answered. "They understand basic commands—come, sit, and stay—better than I thought. I spoke to Jimmy today, and he's willing to come to some of the training sessions. I think he wants to commit to adopting the boys, but the water thing is really important to him, so he's hesitant to get too attached until he sees how it goes."

I leaned over and ruffled Bowie behind the ears. I was awarded with a sloppy kiss. "I think things went well today. Based on the progress we made, I have a feeling we'll have the boys swimming by the end of the week. Which reminds me: Whatever happened with that Newfoundland that was brought in a couple of weeks ago? The one who was found wandering on the highway. Now there was a dog who loved the water."

"I was able to track down his owner, who, as it turned out, had recently passed away. The next of kin didn't want the dog, so I asked a couple of folks I knew who I felt would be good with such a large dog, but those initial inquiries didn't pan out. Eventually, I found him a home near Bigfork that I think is perfect for him. The man who adopted him lives alone in a little cabin on the lake."

I smiled. "That does sound perfect." I loved Brady for taking so much time with the animals he placed. There were those who would adopt the orphans entrusted to them out to anyone willing to take them, but Brady's attitude was that they were better off with him than with the wrong person, and I agreed.

We firmed up plans for Monday, and Tilly and I headed to my Jeep. I wanted to stop at my cabin to pick up a few things to bring to Tony's, and it occurred to me that I might be able to track down Sue Wade at the quilting circle gathering before I went.

Sue's Sewing Nook was next door to the Black Bear Café, and the women in the group met at the store on the first Saturday of every month to work on their latest project for a few hours before going there to have a meal. When I arrived at the café, the group was just breaking up. I indicated to Sue that I needed to speak to her, and she suggested we head next door, where we could speak in private. Tilly was still wet from her morning swim, so I left her in the Jeep with the windows rolled down.

"How can I help you?" Sue asked after unlocking the door and ushering me inside.

"I came across a Mother's Day card that had been sent to Edna Fairchild from someone who signed the card as 'The Prodigal Child.' I'd like to inform this person that Edna has died, so I'm trying to locate them. I've done some research and found out Edna had a son, Chip. It appears you may have known him, and I hoped you'd know how to get hold of him."

Sue narrowed her gaze, appearing hesitant to speak. I decided to wait quietly while she took a moment to process her thoughts. The overhead lights reflected off her now-blond hair as her green eyes honed on something across the shop. I glanced in the same direction but couldn't pick out what she'd been looking at.

At last she began to speak. "I did know Chip. We went to high school together, and while we had friends in common, I wouldn't exactly say we were good friends. I can probably fill in a few blanks for you, though I have no idea how to reach him now."

"Anything you can tell me might help."

Sue sat down on one of the chairs surrounding a large rectangular table, gesturing for me to join her there. The shop was cozy, with a lot of homey accents from the handcrafted goods made by the men and women who frequented the store. My favorite was a tapestry of a bear standing in a flower-covered meadow, with the majestic mountains that framed the area towering behind. It seemed amazing to me that the work felt like a painting but was made entirely from small pieces of fabric sewn together.

I turned my attention to Sue as soon as she began to speak. "His real name was Greg, and he moved to White Eagle during his sophomore year of high school. Although I didn't know why at the time, it was quickly evident he had a chip on his shoulder, which not only earned him his nickname, but also made him something of an outcast."

"What do you mean by a chip on his shoulder?"

"He was prone to explosive anger. Additionally, he was a small kid, several inches shorter than boys his age, so it wasn't surprising he had a hard time making friends. What he seemed to be good at was making enemies; he managed to pile up quite a few of those during the first half year he lived here."

"Any idea where the anger came from?"

Sue nodded. "I didn't know it at the time, although I eventually discovered the fuel that seemed to set the flame. But I'm getting to that. I think you need the background first."

"Of course. I'm sorry. Go ahead."

"During the summer between Chip's sophomore and junior years, one of the local boys took mercy on him and went out of his way to strike up a friendship with him. Having a friend seemed to mellow Chip, and by the time school started in the fall, he had a group of friends and a decent social life."

"Do you remember the name of the person who befriended him?"

"Rupert Hanson."

"Mike spoke to Rupert. He didn't mention knowing Chip's real name or anything about him."

"Rupert is the sort to stay out of things. If Mike spoke to him, he would most likely have answered his questions selectively, and he wouldn't have volunteered anything. I used to think he was being intentionally difficult, but it's just his way to keep what he knows, thinks, and feels close to the vest."

"Okay, back to Chip. He and Rupert became friends…"

"They were, though things were dicey after the gun incident."

I leaned forward slightly. "I found records that suggested Chip was expelled from high school during his senior year for pulling a gun on another student. I assume that's what you mean?"

Sue nodded. "It is. I'm getting to it."

"Of course." I sat back. "Please continue."

"Chip had a growth spurt the summer before his senior year, so by the time school started he was almost six feet tall. He'd begun to settle in and no longer seemed so angry and defensive. I was dating Rupert at the time, although that didn't last long, so for a while I ran into Chip at parties and other gatherings. It seemed as if things were looking up for Chip; then his father ended up in the news and everything went to hell."

"His father?"

"Dorian Fairchild. He was convicted of killing six women in three states the year before Edna and Chip moved to White Eagle."

My hand flew to my mouth. "Oh my God. That's awful."

"It was awful for everyone involved. After Fairchild was convicted, Chip changed his last name, but Edna insisted she'd married the man and was bound to him in good times and bad and refused to give up the name she received on her wedding day. Looking back, I think Edna's insistence on maintaining her marriage to a man who was no better than a monster was at the root of Chip's problems with his mother."

"I guess I can understand that. Chip probably wanted to put that part of his life behind him. His mother's refusal to let go most likely made a totally new start impossible."

Sue nodded. "That might have been at least part of what eventually tore them apart. While they moved to White Eagle with the hope of starting over, Chip couldn't completely deny his father's existence as long as his mother refused to get a divorce."

I took a moment to let that sink in. Wow. Poor Chip. "You said his father ended up in the news. Why?"

"It seemed that as part of his plea deal to avoid the death penalty, he agreed to provide the names and burial sites of all his victims, but there was one victim he didn't admit to killing. An investigator who wouldn't give up on the idea that Fairchild had killed that young woman found the body and was able to demonstrate the similarities between the methods used to kill her and the six women Fairchild had admitted to killing. The media, doing what they do, not only plastered the news with images of Dorian Fairchild, but there were photos of Edna and Chip in all the regional newspapers. When the local kids found out Chip was the son of a serial killer, some of them were less than kind."

I was afraid I could see where this was going, and I didn't like it a bit.

"There was one boy, Larry Jorgenson, who began taunting Chip about having demon blood. It was cruel and uncalled for, but Larry was a big, popular kid, so most of the others didn't do anything to stick up for Chip. Poor Chip's world fell apart. As the taunting continued, he became increasingly angry and withdrawn. He began cutting school, not that I blamed him. I wouldn't have wanted to subject myself to the bullying either."

"Couldn't the school administration do anything to protect Chip from kids like Larry?"

Sue shrugged. "What could they do? Larry was careful not to taunt Chip when teachers were around. It was his word against Larry's, and without proof, there was little anyone could do other than talk to both Larry and his parents, which they did."

"It's so unfair this poor kid had to suffer for the sins of his father."

"I agree. Looking back, I wish I would have done more to help Chip, but I was a kid too, and my instinct was to stay out of things. Anyway, the bullying went on, and Chip became increasingly aggressive. I'm not sure what finally made him snap, but one day in January, he showed up in school with a gun and held it to Larry's head. I'm not sure if he intended to shoot him or if he was just warning him to back off, but his stunt resulted in his being expelled. Chip spent some time in juvie. When he got out, he hooked up with some older kids and started getting into all kinds of trouble. His mom was in over her head, unable to control his actions. They fought constantly. Eventually, Chip left town, and no one in White Eagle has seen him again."

I felt a catch of emotion at the back of my throat. "That's some story."

"It was tragic, really. I can't imagine having to live in the shadow of the horrible man he'd once called Daddy. I hope you can find Chip. I heard his monster of a father died in prison a few years after Chip left town. I suppose that might have allowed him to move on and build another life using, I imagine, another name. The fact that he reached out to Edna after all this time seems significant to me. I'd hate to think he would show up to their special place on Mother's Day only to have her not appear. If he doesn't know she's dead, he'll probably think she refused to forgive him. That would be a tragedy all over again."

"I agree. And I'm going to try to find him. Thanks for sharing all this."

Sue placed her hand on my arm and gave it a squeeze. "No problem. I'm happy to help in any way I can."

While I'd been interested in finding Chip and informing him of his mother's death before, now that I understood his background, my interest had morphed into dogged determination.

Chapter 6

Tony was out in the yard with Titan and the kittens when Tilly and I arrived. The snow had melted in his yard, and I'd noticed when I was there the day before that he'd begun his spring-cleaning, but today it appeared he had something different in mind. His table saw was set up on the deck and there was a pile of wood nearby, as well as bags of soil, mulch, and fertilizer, and gallon cans of what looked to be herbs.

"Planting a garden?" I asked as Tilly ran to Titan with her tail wagging.

"A patio garden. I've been trying to cook more often, rather than going for my traditional menu of frozen pizza and boxed mac and cheese. It occurred to me that it would be both convenient and cost effective to grow my own herbs. I wanted something close to the kitchen, so I decided to build planter boxes on the deck near the slider off the kitchen. If the herbs work out, I may try some tomatoes, and maybe some peppers and carrots as well."

"That's really awesome. I knew you had a few go-to dishes you liked to cook, but I had no idea you knew one herb from another."

Tony raised a brow. "I'm Italian. Of course I can cook."

I laughed. "I wasn't aware that being Italian automatically meant you could cook."

Tony grinned. "I guess the two aren't automatically linked, but my nona is a great cook, and she taught me how to get around in the kitchen at an early age. If you hadn't had to hurry off this morning, I could have made you one of my famous egg-white omelets."

"I don't have anything going on tomorrow, so I could stay over again tonight," I hinted. "In fact, if you want to feed me all weekend, I'd be happy to oblige your culinary urges."

Tony wiped the sweat from his brow with the back of his arm. "That's very generous of you. I might just take you up on that." Tony returned to the boards he was arranging now that he'd cut them to size. "Any dinner requests?"

"How about something Italian? Spaghetti?"

Tony grinned. Streaks of dirt marred his unshaven cheeks as small beads of sweat lingered on his neck. "I can do that. I want to finish this section so I can plant the herbs I've already purchased. You can help if you want."

I tossed the backpack I used for a purse on the picnic table. "Okay. What can I do?"

Tony looked at my feet, which were bare except for flip-flops. "You might want to put on some tennis shoes. I'd hate for you to smash a toe. And maybe long pants so you don't scrape up your legs."

"It's too hot for pants." I looked to Tony's long legs, which were covered in worn jeans that hung low on his hips. The man really did grunge up nice. I was used to Tony being clean-shaven and freshly showered, and his work with computers rarely led to muddy or sweaty streaks. I liked unkempt Tony. Very primal. "I'll go inside and put on tennis shoes. Can I get you something? A beer?"

"A beer would be great."

I paused and glanced back through the sliding glass door as Tony returned to his hammer and nails. It wasn't that I'd never seen him get his hands dirty before, but today he seemed entirely different. I suppose part of me still saw Tony as the nerd I'd first met in the seventh grade, but while he was as smart as he ever was, physically he'd transformed into something so much more. My temperature on the rise, I ran upstairs, grabbed a pair of tennis shoes, pulled them on my feet, and headed down to grab the beers to help Tony turn his back deck into a garden.

For the next few hours, we sawed, nailed, planted, and watered. By the time the sun had curved around to line up for its descent behind the mountain, Tony had a garden that not only softened the harsh lines of the wooden deck but lent a scent to the area that I knew was going to be heavenly throughout the summer. We shared a bottle of wine on the outdoor table, admiring our work, as Titan and Tilly romped on the lawn. I don't think either of us intended to stay out on the deck as long as we did, but after a day of labor, watching the sun set behind the mountain at the far end of the lake while we sipped wine and discussed the most appropriate vegetables to add to the garden boxes that hadn't been planted with herbs seemed just about as perfect an end to a day as I'd experienced in a long time.

After the sun set, we went inside to shower. Separately, of course. It took me longer to deal with washing my long hair, so by the time I joined Tony in the kitchen, he had a pot of spaghetti sauce simmering on the stovetop and a sink full of lettuce, tomatoes, cucumbers, carrots, and radishes, waiting to be washed and chopped for a salad.

I'd put on clean jeans and a T-shirt, but my feet were bare and my hair, still damp, hung down my back. "Something smells wonderful."

"I had sauce in the freezer, so all I had to do was heat it up. And I had bread that just needed to be baked and ingredients for the salad. Wine?"

I knew I should say no. We'd already shared a bottle on the deck, but I wasn't driving home, and wine, especially a red, did bring out the flavor of the sauce I just knew was going to be mouthwatering. "Are you trying to make me light-headed so you can beat me in the game?" I teased.

"Maybe." Tony's eyes sparkled with humor. "Is it working?"

"Not yet, and yes, I'd love some wine." I waited while Tony poured me a glass. "Can I help?"

"I think I've got it. You can sit here on the barstool and talk to me while I cook."

I slipped onto the stool. "I can do that. It was fun helping you today. I've been thinking about doing some renovations to my cabin, but I don't know where to start. I don't have a lot of money to spend, but I feel like my living space needs some work, and now that I've seen your deck, I'm fantasizing about my own patio garden. I'd plant flowers rather than herbs because I don't really cook, but it sure would be nice to look out the window and see a colorful garden every day. Was the wood expensive?"

"Not at all. In fact, I have a lot more than I'll ever use. I considered cutting it up for kindling, but if you want some boxes for your deck, you can use my excess. Maybe I can come by next week and we can get started."

I grinned. "Really? That would be awesome. I'm supposed to meet Brady at the lake on Monday for session two of the terrier swimming project, but Tuesday would work for me."

"Tuesday is fine for me as well. I'll come over early and get set up. Maybe I'll follow you home tomorrow so I can draw up some plans and take some measurements. It'd be easiest to cut the boards here and then bring them to your place ready to install."

"Works for me. And thanks, Tony. This really has been an awesome day."

After he popped the bread into the oven, he put up some water for the noodles to boil and began assembling the salad. I kept up my end of the bargain by chatting about this and that as he worked. Chip's whereabouts and the questions I had for Tony regarding what if any information he might have uncovered since that morning were tickling my mind in a most annoying way, but the day and evening had been so perfect so far, I decided to wait to bring up that subject until after we finished dinner.

I set the table while Tony drained the pasta. After he sliced the bread I found a basket for it, then set the salad bowl in the middle of the table while Tony served up two large plates of pasta and sauce and set them down on the placemats I'd found in the drawer where I thought he kept his napkins.

"So good," I groaned as I took my first bite of the absolutely-to-die-for meat sauce. "I can't believe you had this just lurking in your freezer."

"Most of the time it's just me to eat whatever I make, so I freeze the rest to heat up when I have less time or less inclination to start from scratch."

I took another bite, appreciating the flavors as they tantalized my tongue. "I had no idea. I think raiding your freezer is going to be one of my new routines whenever I come over. Most nights, I settle for canned soup or frozen dinners. And not this sort of frozen dinner. The actual frozen dinners that come in cardboard containers."

After we'd devoured the pasta, bread, and salad, I helped Tony clean up. There was something comforting about putting away leftovers and wiping counters while he loaded the dishwasher. I liked living alone, and most of the time it never occurred to me that doing something as mundane as cleaning the kitchen alongside another person could be so gratifying.

Once the kitchen was clean, we pulled on jackets and wandered outside to give the dogs a bathroom break. It was completely dark now, but Tony had bright deck lights, and the dogs knew not to wander far unless someone was with them.

"I've had the best day and hate to even bring this up, but did you manage to find anything new on Chip's whereabouts?"

"Maybe. I was going to talk to you about some leads that may not wind up anywhere once followed, but like you, the day seemed too perfect to bring up the mystery before now."

"Before you begin, I spoke to Sue Wade. If you remember, she was in the photo you found of the teens standing on the high-school football field in the yearbook. She had some interesting yet alarming things to share." I took the next several minutes to go over everything Sue had told me. Tony's expression grew grim as I described the bullying Chip had suffered at the hands of Larry Jorgenson. By the time I'd shared everything, the dogs had finished their wandering, so we headed inside.

We sat down at the kitchen table to talk things through. Tony had a laptop upstairs, and if we needed more juice we could always go down to the basement, but it seemed easiest to talk upstairs, where we could keep an eye on the animals.

"So, what did you find?" I asked.

Tony sat forward, resting his arms on the table in front of him. "I found evidence that Chip once had a Montana State driver's license under the name Greg Townsend. It expired when he was twenty-one and he never renewed it. I looked for a license in the same name in another state but didn't fine one. I'm not sure why. I suppose it's possible he lost his license for some reason; maybe he had a DUI or some other infraction that would lead to a suspension of his license. Or he might have been incarcerated, although I haven't found a criminal record for him after he left White Eagle. He could have been out of the country, or he may have changed his name. It's hard to say at this point."

"How do we find him if he doesn't even have a driver's license? What about social security records?"

"I'm looking into his work history as Greg. So far, I haven't found anything, which leads me to believe he either changed his name or left the country, as I suggested, but it's early yet. I'm sure something will pop eventually."

"It seems pretty strange that he simply disappeared. Who does that these days?"

"It's possible he stole an identity or has been living off the radar using an alias. Maybe he got tired of people making the connection between him and his father, so he might have changed his name without bothering to go through the court system to make it legal. If he did steal an identity, there wouldn't be a paper trail to follow."

"If he changed his name, I don't see how we'll ever find him," I groaned.

Tony shrugged. "It's too soon to give up. I figure I'll widen my search criteria for Greg Townsend. If I don't find anything, we might need to consider the alias idea."

I sat back in my chair and considered the situation. Who knew it would be so hard to find him given today's technology? Everyone, it seemed, was linked to the internet in one way or another and easily found via a simple Google search. "Maybe we should change gears a bit. We've been looking for Chip, but maybe we should be looking for people who knew him. If we can't find clues to where he might have been in the last twenty-five years, maybe we can find a relative or family friend he stayed in touch with."

Tony stretched out his long legs. "You said he was relatively happy and settled between his junior year of high school and December of his senior year, when his father showed up in the news. Did he have a girlfriend?"

I shrugged. "I have no idea. Why do you ask?"

"It just seems a girlfriend could be someone he'd open up to. Not about his father or his past, but maybe about a positive childhood memory, like an uncle who took him camping or a grandfather who had a cabin at the lake. That sort of thing. If Chip had a family member he continued to stay in touch with, that might be our best bet at finding him."

"I didn't ask Sue about a girlfriend when I spoke to her today, but I will." I glanced at the clock. "It's sort of late to call now. I'll do it in the morning."

Tony clapped his hands together. "We've done what we can for tonight. How about we finish that video game while I have you relaxed and pliant from the wine."

I laughed. "In your dreams. A little wine isn't going to slow me down one bit. You should know by now that my killer instinct never goes dormant. I was pretty close to beating you last night and most likely would have if it hadn't been so late."

Tony stood up, reached out a hand, and pulled me to my feet. "Okay, my little terminator. Let's see what you've got. Would you care to make a wager?"

"How about a buck?" I figured a dollar was all I could afford to lose.

Tony locked eyes with me. "How about something more personal?"

I felt a catch in my throat. "Personal?"

Tony used a finger to brush a stray lock of hair behind my ear. "Loser gives the winner a shoulder rub."

I let out a breath. A shoulder rub sounded innocent enough. "Deal. I could use a shoulder rub after all that lifting and hauling today. In fact, I'm pretty sore. I hope you have enough energy left after our long day to get in there deep and work out those kinks."

Tony began to cough. He picked up his water and took a drink. "Trust me. I'm good with kinks."

Chapter 7

Sunday, May 6

I woke the next morning to an empty room. Tilly and the kittens had slept with me, so the fact that they weren't there now seemed to indicate Tony was already up and had let them out. I glanced out the window and smiled. It was another beautiful day. Sunshine and plenty of it, by the look of things. I put my arms over my head and stretched. It was nice to have a day every now and then when there were no demands on my time requiring me to wake by a certain hour. I was momentarily tempted to snuggle back in and sleep for another half hour, but the smell of cinnamon and coffee began to penetrate my sleep-clogged mind.

"Um," I said aloud after inhaling deeply. Coffee did seem pretty wonderful, and cinnamon? Unless my sense of smell was off completely, it seemed Tony was baking something sweet. Cinnamon rolls? Cinnamon bread? Suddenly, I had to know.

I peeled back the covers and sat up on the side of the bed. I looked around the room. I'd chosen this room because of the color that first time I'd stayed over. Tony had told me to pick any room I wanted, so I'd wandered around to find just the right one. I loved the way the light gray walls trimmed with white crown molding provided an earthy contrast to the furniture, which was hardwood. The color of the tall, majestic bed matched the flooring: a dark wood that seemed to bring the feel of the forest indoors. The deep blue comforter on the king bed contrasted nicely with the light blue sheets and dark blue pillowcases.

I glanced out the window again at the sun shimmering on the lake in the distance. The view from this room was spectacular too. It appeared we were going to be in for another warm day, so I pulled on a pair of denim shorts, a white tank top, and a dark blue sweatshirt, then headed to the attached bathroom. I brushed my teeth and washed up a bit, then went downstairs.

"What smells so wonderful?" I asked as Tony handed me a hot cup of coffee in a sturdy stoneware mug.

"Apple cinnamon muffins. I wanted to make blueberry, but I'm out of berries. I'll stop by the farmers market while we're out today."

"We're going out?" I asked after petting Tilly, who had abandoned her spot on the floor next to Titan to greet me.

Tony poured cracked and beaten eggs into a pan and began to scramble them. "It occurred to me that it might be beneficial to speak to the folks at the assisted-living facility where Edna lived before she passed. We talked about the fact that Chip might have stayed in touch with a relative or family friend. Maybe Edna mentioned such a person to someone she met while living there. I know it's a long shot, but it's a lovely day and a drive to Kalispell would be nice anyway."

I walked over to the window and looked out. Tang had caught sight of me and wandered into the kitchen with Tinder on his tail. I set down my coffee and picked up both kittens for a cuddle, rubbing their soft fur against my face as they began to purr. Then I put them down, picked up my coffee, and turned back to Tony. "It's a nice day and a drive would be relaxing. We can bring the dogs and stop at the lake. Do you think the assisted-living facility will allow us to just pop in and start talking to folks?"

Tony stirred the eggs. "I called ahead and explained who I was and what I wanted. The woman I spoke to said it would be fine to come by and speak to the staff and residents who may have known Edna if we stayed in the common areas. She thought with the nice weather a lot of the residents would want to spend time out on the patio, which seems like as good a spot as any to start. She also said it would be best to come by before lunch. A lot of the residents nap in the afternoon. I told her we'd probably be there around ten-thirty."

"Chip said he wanted to meet Edna in their 'special spot' on Mother's Day. We should ask about that." I took a sip of my coffee. I felt the warmth slide down my throat. Heaven.

"Chances are, the spot Chip referred to is in or close to White Eagle," Tony added. "It might be a good idea to talk to some of Edna's local friends as well. She might have shared a fond memory with them when she lived here."

I walked over to the counter and leaned my elbows against it. "Patty Paulson owns the trinket shop next to Bree's bookstore, which used to be Edna's antique store. I think she's about the same age as Edna was, so they might have been friends. We can stop in to chat with her."

"Is she open on Sunday?" Tony scooped fluffy eggs onto a platter.

"She is. The shop is closed on Mondays and Tuesdays. Let's drop by on our way to Kalispell. I think she opens at nine and closes at three on Sundays, so we might be too late to catch her by the time we get back."

Tony slid the muffins out of the oven and set them on a hot pad, then transferred them to a plate and set that on the table next to the eggs. After adding a bowl of strawberries with whipped cream to the table, he went back for the coffeepot and topped off our mugs. He made certain I had everything I needed before sitting down across from me.

"I was really in the mood for blueberry, but these apple cinnamon muffins turned out well," Tony said after taking a bite.

"They're delicious. Is that nutmeg and maybe some allspice I taste?"

Tony nodded. "I used several spices in addition to the cinnamon to give it more of a kick; ginger and cloves, as well as a few other things. I'd like to try this same recipe with peaches or apricots rather than apples. The farmers market should begin having a wider selection of summer fruit in a month or so."

"They have that big farmers market in Kalispell on the weekends. Maybe we should stop by. Between our planting yesterday and this talk of summer fruits, I'm suddenly in the mood for some fresh produce. The larger market has a much better selection than our little local one."

Tony took a bite of his eggs. "Other than the assisted-living facility, Patty's trinket shop, and the farmers market, is there anywhere else you want to go today?"

"I still need to call Sue Wade. If she remembers Chip having a girlfriend in high school, I might try to track her down. Other than that, I can't think of anyone Chip might have confided in about a favorite relative or childhood memory. It seems to me that guys don't talk with one another about that sort of thing."

"Not generally," Tony agreed. He dipped a strawberry in the whipped cream, then popped it into his mouth. He chewed slowly before continuing. "Still, under the right set of circumstances, he might share that sort of memory with a friend. Maybe someone who'd experienced something similar."

"Perhaps. So, how about you? Do you have a favorite relative or childhood memory?"

Tony smiled. He took a second strawberry and repeated the dipping-and-eating process. "Absolutely."

"And would you be willing to share those memories with this friend?"

He grinned. "I'll show you mine if you show me yours."

I laughed. "Assuming you're being provocative to tease and don't intend for us to show anything in a literal sense, I'll swap memories with you, but you go first."

"Very well. My favorite relative is my grandmother, who I refer to as Nona. She lives in a small village in northern Italy, and she's the best cook in the entire world."

"She's your favorite because she's a good cook?"

"Partially. But it's more than that. When I was young my parents were frustrated by my intelligence. I didn't understand it then, but now I can see they weren't sure what to do with me, and I guess I caused them some grief with my behavior problems in school. That drove a wedge between us."

"You were bored, and probably frustrated," I said.

Tony looked surprised. "Exactly. The adults in my life—my parents and teachers— understood the bored part. Their solution to my classroom misbehavior was to have me read a book while the rest of the class completed math worksheets that took them an hour but me only a few minutes. I guess I can see why they might consider that a good solution, but what they didn't get was that I wasn't just bored, I was frustrated. I had a voracious appetite for knowledge. I wanted to be challenged. I wanted to learn new things, but my parents didn't want to send me to a school for gifted students or have me placed in an accelerated learning program. They wanted me to go to a normal school with kids my own age, so I'd have a normal life. The problem was, the teachers who taught my classes, to which I was assigned purely based on my age, didn't have anything to teach me that I didn't already know. I felt stifled and stagnant. As I got older and smarter, I became increasingly frustrated, so I acted out."

"And Nona could challenge you?"

"She did, although not in the way I really yearned to be challenged. She wasn't a genius and she couldn't talk to me about math or computers, but she knew how to do things I didn't, so she taught them to me. She taught me to cook and to weave. She taught me to map the stars and to speak Italian. She taught me about gardening and irrigation systems, and she even taught me to read and understand the great philosophers. My parents worked a lot of hours when I was in grade school, so every summer, I was sent to stay with Nona. Those were the best summers of my life."

"Do you still visit?"

"Every chance I get. I was just in Italy last month for a week, and I plan to go back for a couple of weeks over the summer."

I sat back in my chair. "I'd love to meet your nona someday. She sounds wonderful. And if you learned to cook from her, I'd love to try her cooking. I don't like to cook, but I love to eat."

Tony appeared thoughtful. "And I'd love for you to meet her." He took a sip of his coffee. "She can be picky when it comes to the women in my life, but I think she'd like you."

"The women in your life? Have you taken many to meet her?"

"No, but she has a way of keeping an eye on me even from a distance. So, how about you? Do you have a favorite relative or childhood memory?"

I paused for a moment to think about that. I didn't have a lot of relatives, but I was very fond of the ones I did. "I think all my relatives are my favorite in one way or another. My mom is nurturing, and encouraging, and so very special to me, and Aunt Ruthie was such a rock to Mom, Mike, and me after Dad died, or I guess I should say, after he disappeared. Mike can be a tool at times, but overall he's a fantastic brother, and even my cousin Jimmy is an okay guy."

"How about a favorite memory?" Tony encouraged.

"I think I'd have to say that was a fishing trip I took with my dad when I was around six or seven." I felt a warmth in my heart toward my father now that I hadn't since I'd learned he probably hadn't died but had been living a secret life all these years. "Every summer, Dad and Mike took a fishing trip. They went up to Rock Lake to stay at my uncle's cabin for a week. I remember wanting to go so badly, but it was a father-son thing and girls weren't allowed. Then, one summer, just before the trip, Mike got sick. Dad was going to go alone, but I managed to talk him in to letting me go in Mike's place. It was a magical seven days. We cooked over a campfire, fished, hiked, and swam. It was the best week of my life."

"That sounds pretty wonderful."

I smiled. "It was. Of course, after having this wonderful experience and really knowing what I was missing, I was twice as mad the following summer when I was once again left at home while Mike got to go with Dad. There were times when being a girl and the youngest really sucked."

"Didn't you do special mother-daughter things with your mom?" Tony asked.

I shrugged. "Mom tried to find things for us to do together, but we weren't on the same page. She liked to cook and sew, and I liked to hike and fish." I paused to let the memories wash over me. "Looking back, I think I hurt her feelings when I refused to learn to do the things she loved, but I found the whole home-and-hearth thing so boring. Do you know, my mom makes her own candles and enjoys doing crafts? Me, I want to be outside, hiking, swimming, and skiing, not indoors doing what feels like nothing more than extra chores."

Tony put his hand over mine. I could see understanding and sympathy in his eyes. "It's hard when your parents have a different plan for your life than you do, but in my case, it all worked out."

"What do you mean?"

"As I said, I wanted very badly to be allowed to attend a school for gifted students, where I knew I would be challenged intellectually and hoped to find peers with whom I could find common ground. My parents discussed allowing me to apply for a gifted program when I entered middle school, but then, at the last minute, they changed their mind and decided to move the family instead. When we moved to White Eagle, I thought my life was over. It was even smaller than the town where we'd been living. I realized I not only wasn't going to get the education I craved but moving also meant I didn't have any friends. As you remember, I was pretty much an outcast when I first started school here."

"I remember the kids at school were pretty brutal. I was pretty mean to you in the beginning too."

"Maybe. But you were different. You had a hunger. A drive. I knew from the moment I met you that we were going to play an important role in each other's lives. In the end, it all worked out, and I consider the move to White Eagle to be one of the most important events of my life."

"Why?"

"If my parents hadn't moved us here, I would never have met you, and I think that would have been tragic."

"Aw, Tony." I grasped his hand. "That's so sweet. And you know you mean a lot to me too. I'm sorry your parents didn't provide you with the education you craved, but I'm not sorry they moved here. You really are one of my very best friends, and I trust you more than anyone in my life. You certainly are the only one who knows all my secrets."

Tony started to lean forward. I had the oddest feeling he was going to kiss me, but then he simply wiped a piece of muffin from the corner of my mouth. "We should get these dishes done and get going. We have a busy day ahead."

I nodded, both relieved and disappointed that Tony hadn't been leaning in for a kiss. He was a friend, and it would be much too big a risk for us to become romantically involved, but there were times I wondered how it would feel to be kissed by him. Would it be familiar, comforting, and pleasant, like a hand-quilted comforter wrapped around me on a cold winter day? Or would it be hot, passionate, and consuming, like a forest fire raging out of control?

Chapter 8

After we cleaned up the kitchen, I called Sue to ask her if Chip had had a girlfriend in high school. She said he'd dated a girl named Connie Payton through most of his junior year. Sue and Connie had been friends and had stayed in touch. Now, Connie lived in Polson, on the southern end of Flathead Lake, which was only about an hour's drive from Kalispell. I called her, explained who I was, and asked if it would be all right if Tony and I stopped by later that day. She told me that she'd be working at the café she owned until six, so it was fine to come by at any time before then and gave me directions there.

I got off the phone and took the dogs out for a quick walk. It was still my plan to bring them with us, but it looked like we were going to be spending more time in Tony's truck than we'd originally thought. I wanted to wear them out a bit before we left.

I hadn't decided what to do about the kittens, but after thinking things over, I realized it would be best to drop them and my Jeep off at the cabin on the way out of town. I wouldn't be staying over with Tony again that night because I had work the next day, and it would save me time to have him drop me off at home when we arrived back in town. Besides, he wanted to take measurements for my deck garden, a project I'd become excited about.

When the dogs and I got back to the house, I explained my plan to Tony. It would take him a few minutes to grab the tools he'd need to measure and design my planter boxes, so I left Tilly with him, grabbed the kittens, and headed home. When I arrived, there was a message from Mike on my answering machine.

"Hey, Tess. I wanted to let you know I put some additional feelers out on Chip Townsend. I don't have anything so far, but I'll keep looking. On another subject, I invited Bree to your place for the barbecue on Sunday. She mentioned she didn't have plans for Mother's Day when we had dinner on Friday, so I asked Mom if she minded and she didn't. I assumed that would be okay with you. I'm going fishing today, but I'll be in the office tomorrow and will talk to you then."

"Okay," I said to Tang, who was sitting on the counter watching me as I listened to the message. "What do I need to grab for the day? A change of clothes? A jacket just in case we don't get home until late?"

"Meow."

"You're right. A pair of tennis shoes would be a good idea if I'm wearing flip-flops." I shooed the kitten off the counter, filled the food and water bowls, and checked the litter box, which was perfectly clean.

I'd just finished gathering the things I'd decided I needed when Tony's truck pulled up.

He thought it would be best to do the measurements for the planter boxes now, in case it was dark when we returned to town.

"I'd like something that borders the deck here and here." I pointed to the area I had in mind. "I won't need anything as wide as yours because I just want to plant some colorful annuals, but I'd like the boxes to be long enough to reach all the way down to the end of the back edge of the deck."

Tony pulled out a pad and pencil and drew a quick sketch that exactly matched the image in my head. Once we agreed on size and placement, he took some measurements and promised to get started cutting the wood the following day. Then we loaded Tilly and Titan in the truck and headed into town.

The first stop along our proposed route was Patty's Trinkets, a colorful store that sold a little bit of everything and attracted tourists looking for handcrafted items to take home as souvenirs of White Eagle. I wasn't sure exactly how long Patty had been in business, but I knew it must be well before Edna had closed her antique shop and moved away. I hoped they'd shared memories in the years they'd been neighbors.

"Morning, Tess, Tony. How can I help you today?" Patty asked as she came into the main room from the back in response to the little bell over the door announcing our arrival.

"We wanted to ask you some questions about Edna Fairchild, if that's okay," I said.

Patty nodded. "Bree told me about the card that went to her place. I figured you might be by if you hadn't been able to track down her boy. I wish I could tell you that I knew what had become of him, but Edna didn't like to talk about the past. I didn't even know she had a child until she mentioned him in passing after I'd been operating from this location at least five years."

I leaned my forearms on the counter. "Did she ever mention any other relatives? Maybe someone she stayed in touch with over the years?"

Patty paused, then slowly shook her head. "Not that I can recall. I'm not sure what happened in her past, but I think it must have been pretty bad. Something she wanted to forget. Edna stayed very much in the present. I remember chatting with her a few times around the holidays, and while I shared memories, she never said a word about anything that went back more than a few years." Patty frowned. "Although..."

"Although...?" I prodded gently.

"She did mention someone, now that I think about it. I was telling her about the fun my brother and I had when we were kids living on our grandparents' farm. We were close as children and still are to this day. Edna snorted, then said the only memories she had of her brother were of abandonment and betrayal."

"Did she mention her brother's name?"

"Not that I remember. I suppose there might be records you could look up that would give you that information. I seem to remember Edna said she was born in a small town in Kansas. Cottonwood Falls; I think she said she was from Cottonwood Falls."

"Thanks." I glanced at Tony. "We might be able to use that to track down her brother if he's still alive. I appreciate you taking the time to chat with us."

After that, we headed toward Kalispell. It was a beautiful day, and Tony rolled down the windows so we could enjoy the fresh air.

"You know," I said, "when we were speaking to Patty, it occurred to me that it might be helpful to find out Edna's next of kin. The assisted-living facility might be able to tell us who that is."

"We can certainly ask. Did you bring the card Chip sent to Edna?"

"I did. I figured we might need it to gain cooperation from anyone who might doubt our intentions."

"That's exactly what I was thinking."

I took a deep breath of the fresh spring air as we headed down the highway. Part of me wished we had nothing to do on a day as perfect as this but hike through the wildflowers, swim in the lake, and picnic under a big shade tree. When was the last time I'd had a day with absolutely nothing to do but relax? It had been a while.

I turned and looked at Titan and Tilly. They sat on opposite sides of the backseat with their heads out the windows closest to them, their mouths open and tongues hanging. They looked so content. I stuck my own head out my window and closed my eyes. It was pretty spectacular to have the wind whip through my hair as Bon Jovi blared from the stereo speakers.

Of course, by the time we reached Kalispell my hair looked like rats were nesting in it. I rolled up my window, pulled a brush from my backpack, and began working out the knots.

"Do you have an address for the facility?" Tony asked me.

I looked at the piece of paper I'd used to jot down my notes and rattled it off. Tony punched it into his GPS app and followed the directions.

The facility was smallish compared to some. We learned it housed just twelve residents, each with their own bedroom, bathroom, and kitchenette. Meals were served in a communal dining room if the residents preferred, and there were scheduled activities throughout the day for those who were interested. There was a park just down the street, and we let the dogs out for a minute before we headed inside. It had only been an hour since we'd loaded them into the truck, but we weren't sure how long we'd be inside, so it seemed best to let the dogs stretch their legs a bit before we went in.

We played fetch for twenty minutes, then parked the truck in the shade and rolled down all four windows so the dogs had plenty of air. They were tired from our romp and immediately settled down to nap.

"Can I help you?" a woman in a neat but casual outfit asked as we walked through the front door of the last home Edna had before her death.

"I'm Tony Marconi. I called earlier about speaking to staff and residents who might have known Edna Fairchild."

The woman smiled. "Of course. My name is Helen Short. Why don't you come into my office so we can chat?"

We followed the woman, who appeared to be in her late forties, into a small office. She sat down on one side of a small conference table and indicated chairs for us on the other.

"You mentioned a letter…?"

I took out the card and handed it to her. "Bree Price owns a bookstore that's in the building that used to hold Edna's Antiques. She received the card with her stack of mail and didn't realize it wasn't meant for her until after she opened it. I'm the mail carrier in White Eagle, so she asked me if I could return the card to the sender. The problem is, there was no name or return address on the envelope. I've since learned Edna had a son, Chip. Actually, his legal name was Greg Townsend. We've been trying to find him, but we haven't had any luck so far. We hoped Edna might have spoken to someone during her time here about her son or another relative who might be able to put us in touch with him. As you can see by the letter, it appears he doesn't know she's passed."

She frowned. "Yes, that does appear to be the case." She looked up from the card, which she still held in her hand. "It would be a shame if Edna's son went to their special place after all this time and she wasn't there to meet him. I applaud your efforts to find him. I pulled Edna's records after Mr. Marconi's call. I'm afraid Edna never mentioned having a son. She listed Beth Wright as her emergency contact. I have a phone number I'd be willing to share with you, but I don't know if it's still accurate. The number was provided when Edna moved in and was never updated."

"A phone number would be great," I said.

"Did Edna have any visitors while she lived here?" Tony asked.

"Sadly, no. She didn't make a lot of friends either. She tended to stay in her room, rarely coming down to communal meals or to participate in any of the group activities. There was one resident she talked to from time to time: Warren Cole. He's been with us for ten years and has a way of breaking through the walls of defense that even the most unsocial of our residents occasionally erect."

"Is he here now?" I asked.

"He's on the patio. I'll introduce you."

Tony and I followed Ms. Short through the tidy facility. Just off the dining area was an electric door that led out onto the patio. Helen greeted the residents as we made her way to a tall man sitting in a wheelchair, reading a book.

"Warren, I'd like you to meet Tess and Tony. They're friends of Edna's and would like to speak to you for a few minutes."

His face lit up like a Christmas tree. "I'd love to have some company. Please, have a seat."

Tony and I sat down on nearby patio chairs and briefly summed up our reason for being there, then gave him the card to read.

"Edna had a tough life," he said. "She didn't like to talk about her past, but she did mention a place she liked to go when she needed to relax. I don't know if it's the same place she went with her son, but it might be."

"I agree. Do you remember the name of the place?"

Mr. Cole scrunched up his face. "It was a falls. Not far from her home in White Eagle." He tapped the side of his head with an index finger. "Whispering Falls; that's it. Edna said there was a path that wound around behind the falls. There was a cave or an underground tunnel that allowed you to see the falls from the back side. She told me few people, even locals, knew about it, so it was the perfect place to go when she needed to be alone."

I'd heard of Whispering Falls and had even hiked there a time or two, but I'd never heard there was a way to get around to the back. Whether this was the special place Chip spoke of or not, I was intrigued.

"Is there anything else you can think of that might help us?" I asked.

Mr. Cole shook his head. "Edna lived very much in the now. By the time most folks end up here, the focus of their attention is on the past, but not Edna. She didn't want to remember what had gone on before; she'd learned to keep her sights on the present and only the present. I certainly hope you find the boy who sent the card. It would be a tragedy if he went through the rest of his life believing he'd reached out to his mother and she hadn't accepted his gesture."

"Yes," I said. "It would be a tragedy."

Chapter 9

The first thing I did after Tony and I returned to the truck was to call Beth Wright, Edna's emergency contact. Unfortunately, the phone had been disconnected and there wasn't a forwarding number, so I called Mike and left a message. "I know you're fishing, Mike, but I have a couple of things I need you to follow up on when you get into the office tomorrow. First, I spoke to a woman at the assisted-living facility where Edna lived when she passed, and she gave me the name of Edna's emergency contact. Her name is Beth Wright, but the phone number on file has been disconnected. I have the old number, if that will help you track her down." I rattled off the number. "And I wondered if you could check with the police in Kalispell to see if they contacted anyone else as next of kin when Edna died. Tony and I are following up on some other leads today, but I'd like to keep the momentum going, in case our leads don't pan out. I'd really like to find Edna's son before Mother's Day."

I hung up and turned to Tony. "Okay, let's head to Polson. Connie Payton owns a diner, so we can grab some lunch while we're there. Maybe we can head to the lake and let the dogs take a nice long swim after that."

Tony started the truck. "Seems like a good plan. Rock or country?" he asked, his hand near the radio tuner.

"Rock," I replied as I rolled down all the windows and sang along at the top of my lungs. I giggled when Titan began to howl. I wasn't sure if he was joining in, or if he was trying to let me know my singing was the worst and I should take it down a decibel or two.

The trip to Polson was uneventful. When we arrived at the diner we saw the patio was open, and well-behaved dogs, it seemed, were welcome to dine with their humans. Selecting a table in the shade, Tony instructed both dogs to get down under the table while I went inside to look for Connie Payton. It was lunchtime and so somewhat crowded, but she handed me glasses filled with water and promised to come outside to speak to us as soon as she was able.

"Maybe we should have been more careful about our timing," I said when I returned to Tony and the dogs.

"Is she too busy to speak to us?"

"She said she'd be out. In the meantime, I snagged us a couple of menus. We may as well put in our order while we're waiting."

I ordered a club sandwich and Tony chose a tri-tip sandwich. We both ordered sides of fruit and glasses of ice tea. Shortly after the waitress put in our order, Connie came out to join us.

"I guess we came at the worst possible time," I apologized.

"It's fine. I have plenty of help today." Connie looked under the table. "You have well-behaved dogs."

"My mom owns a restaurant, so they know the drill."

"Would you like something to eat before we get started?"

"We've already ordered," I said. "We'll try to be quick; we can see you're busy."

I handed her Chip's card, then explained what sort of information we hoped she'd be able to provide. I could see reading the card affected her deeply. More so, I was certain, than anyone else who'd read it to this point.

"I guess you know about Chip's father."

I nodded. "Sue Wade filled me in. I can't imagine having to live with something like that. It must have been awful."

"It was. And when he ended up in the news and everyone found out about Chip's relationship to him, it became a whole lot worse. His mother was dealing with things in her own way, but I can tell you with complete certainty they didn't see eye to eye on what was best. I wasn't surprised when he took off. White Eagle had become a cruel place for him."

"Did you stay in contact with him after he left?" I asked.

She shook her head. "Chip changed after the news about his father became public. He was angry and aggressive, and I went from being in love with him to being afraid of him. I broke things off and did my best to stay off his radar. I don't think he stayed in touch with anyone after he left, and then maybe four or five years ago, he called me from out of the blue and apologized for being such a jerk when all I'd wanted to do was help him through a difficult time. He sounded like the old Chip. The one I fell in love with."

"Did he give you a way to contact him?"

She tilted her head. "No. And I didn't ask. I was glad Chip called. It brought me closure. But he hadn't been part of my life for a very long time. I was married with children of my own by the time he reached out, and I'd moved from White Eagle and owned this restaurant. I wasn't interested in renewing our friendship."

"That's understandable." I nodded toward the card on the table. "Chip mentions meeting his mother at their 'special place.' Do you know where that might be?"

She furrowed her brow. "I can't say I know for certain, but I do remember him telling me that shortly after they arrived in White Eagle, he and his mom went out hiking and found a tunnel leading to an open area behind a water fall."

"Whispering Falls?"

She nodded. "I think so. He only mentioned it once, when he was in a particularly sentimental mood, but that sounds right. He also mentioned a lake that was special to him and his mother, but I can't remember the name. I had a feeling it was a place they visited when he was a child, so it might not be anywhere around here."

"Did Chip ever talk about a relative he was close to?"

She shook her head. "He didn't talk about family."

"I understand his mother had a brother. Did he ever mention an uncle?"

She sat back and looked up at the sky. "Not an uncle specifically, but I remember him talking about someone who was around when he was a kid. Another adult besides his parents he spent time with. Georgie, I think. He said Georgie taught him to shoot a gun, and he wished he had his gun with him when he found out what his father had done." She lowered her eyes. "Being a teenager is tough anyway, but being a teenager and having to deal with that must have been unbearable."

"Yeah," I agreed. I was sure it was.

She needed to get back to work, so Connie Payton said her good-byes just before our food was delivered. The sandwiches were fantastic, piled high with homemade bread and fresh ingredients. If the restaurant wasn't so far away, this would definitely be a place I'd come back to.

After we finished, we loaded up the dogs and drove back toward White Eagle.

"It's still early," I said as we sped north, "and it's light late into the day now. I bet we'd have time to hike up to Whispering Falls to look around."

"Have you ever been there?" Tony asked.

"A few times when I was a kid. I didn't know about the secret passage, but I remember where the trailhead is. It's been a while, but I think it's only a mile or two from the parking area."

"I wouldn't mind a hike. I bet the dogs would like to stretch their legs too. We'll need to skip the farmers market, though."

I shrugged. "We can catch it next weekend."

"Do you have everything you need?" Tony asked. He looked at my feet. "Other shoes?"

I nodded. "In my pack. I have a change of clothes and a jacket as well."

The parking area was littered with cars here and there. During the summer, you had to arrive early to even get a spot, but the tourist season had yet to kick in and a lot of the locals were busy with spring-cleaning and outdoor projects at this time of the year. I changed into my tennis shoes, added water and granola bars and the dogs' leashes to a small day pack Tony had stashed under his seat, and headed down the well-marked trail with Tony at my side and Tilly and Titan trotting before us.

"Look at the flowers!" I gasped in delight as we passed a large meadow with green grass crowded with red, yellow, and purple flowers. It was kept damp by a rambling brook, so I imagined it was lush and green most of the year.

"Beautiful," Tony agreed. "Maybe I'll come back with my camera. My real camera," he specified. "Not just my phone."

"I'd love to take a photo of the meadow and blow it up for that big wall next to the fireplace in my cabin. I'd put it in one of those rustic wooden frames, stained dark to bring out the colors. The textures."

"Any particular angle you'd choose?"

I stopped walking and scanned the meadow, looking for the perfect perspective. The snow on the mountains beyond seemed to magnify the green of the grass and the colors of the wildflowers. "There." I pointed to the remnants of an old log cabin.

"That would make a good shot, all right." Tony looked up the trail. "I think we'd better keep going. We'll need to hurry if we want to have time to look around when we get to the falls."

The trail was well marked but narrow and rocky. It was steep in places, with switchbacks as it wound its way up the mountain. Small seasonal creeks trickled across the hard-packed dirt in places, requiring detours through the brush if we didn't want to deal with making the rest of the hike with wet shoes.

We paused only twice, once to take a sip from our water bottles and once to watch a deer family as they made their way toward the river, which sounded as if it was off to our right. Even with our steady pace, it took almost ninety minutes to reach the base of the falls.

"It's farther than I remembered," I said when we paused to consider the raging flow of water from the seasonal runoff.

"And the trail wasn't an easy one, even for seasoned hikers like us," Tony added.

I took a swig of my water, then wiped my mouth with the back of my arm. "You're thinking there's no way Chip would ask his mother, who had to have been in her late sixties when she died, to meet him all the way up here."

"The thought crossed my mind," Tony acknowledged. "Even if, like you, Chip hadn't remembered the distance, if he came here often, he'd have remembered the steep incline. He also would have realized the falls would be full in the spring. If there's a way to sneak behind them, I suspect that access is only available in late summer and fall."

I let my eyes take in the scene before me. The gushing water flowing over the edge of the mountain into the lake below was beautiful, but at this time of year, it was also loud and dangerous.

"You're right. It doesn't make sense. Even if Chip didn't know about Edna's health issues, he would have no reason to believe she was in good enough shape to make the climb. He must be referring to a different special place. Somewhere accessible." I groaned. "In other words, we're back to square one."

"Seems like it."

I tilted my head up to the sky. It had taken us a lot longer than I'd anticipated to make it this far. "We should start back. I don't want to get caught out here once the sun goes down."

"Agreed." Tony took my hand in his and we started back down the trail we'd just climbed. "After that big lunch I didn't think I'd even want dinner, but with all this exercise, I'm starving."

"We can stop to pick something up on our way back through town. Maybe open a bottle of wine and eat our takeout on my deck. Watch the sunset."

"Sounds like a plan. Let's try that new Chinese place. I hear it's good."

"I like Chinese."

We walked silently for the next twenty minutes or so. It was a beautiful day, and even if we hadn't found the special spot Chip had referred to in his card, I wasn't unhappy that we'd come. I felt like we were making progress, though any time I really thought about things, I realized we were no further along than when we started. If we wanted to find

Chip before Mother's Day, we were running out of time, and that frustrated me. I wasn't the sort to tolerate being frustrated. I let out a breath and then changed my line of thought by bringing up another frustrating subject. "Do you have any news on my mom's Italian lover?"

"Not really. I spoke to my contact and hope to hear from him in a week or two."

"A week or two?"

"I figured there wasn't any urgency, because, as we discussed, your mom is here and Romero is in Italy. My friend is a busy man; I didn't want to push for something faster if I didn't have to."

I supposed that made sense. "And my dad? Any news about him?"

Tony shook his head. "After that first couple of hits there hasn't been anything. It's possible we just got lucky with what we found in December and February, and the expectation of continued hits was unrealistic. It's more likely, though, that someone found out I was looking into things and tightened security."

"We keep talking about *someone* doing this and *someone* doing that. Who's this *someone*?" I asked, a hint of frustration in my voice.

"I don't know. I wish I did. Knowing who's behind this would make the search for answers easier. At this point, I'm just taking stabs in the dark with the hope of hitting something."

I ran my hands through my hair. "This whole thing is so absurd. My dad was a regular guy. He went to work, came home, watched television, drank beer, and, two or three times a year, went fishing. Sure, he was away from home a lot given the nature

103

of his job, but it never felt like he was sneaking around. The idea that he could be a spy or involved with some covert group is beginning to seem more and more ridiculous."

"I know."

"And the hardest part is not knowing if he's a good guy or a bad guy. Even if he's a spy, who is he spying for? And if he's part of some black ops group, is he working for Uncle Sam or someone else? And why the ruse? If he had a job like that, why on earth did he get married and have children? Based on what we've found, it seems he would have to have been involved long before he married my mom or had Mike and me."

Tony laced his fingers with mine and faced me. "I don't have answers to your questions. All I can say is that I'll continue to look until you have them."

I leaned forward and laid my head on his chest.

Tony tightened his arm around me and held me tight. Then he stepped back. "Okay?"

I nodded.

"Let's go get that takeout. My stomach hasn't stopped rumbling since we talked about food."

Chapter 10

Monday, May 7

"Mornin', Hap," I greeted Hap Hollister as Tilly and I entered his home and hardware store to drop off his mail. He'd lived in White Eagle for as long as anyone could remember and had a relaxed way about him that eased any tension I was carrying around on any given day.

"Tess; Tilly. Looks like we're in for another beautiful day."

"It should be gorgeous all week," I said as I placed his stack of mail on the counter. "This wonderful weather has me in the mood to dive into an outdoor project or two. Do you still have paint on sale?"

Hap nodded. "Clear through Memorial Day. You thinking of painting something?"

I grinned. "Planter boxes. I was at Tony's this weekend, and he made some for his deck. He stained his a natural wood color, which looks nice, and I thought I might stain mine as well, but I stopped by the secondhand store this morning and stumbled onto a rocker exactly like the one I'd been dreaming of for my deck. I had the clerk hold it for me because I couldn't very well take it while I was in the middle of my route, but all morning I've been wondering how that rocker would look painted a pretty blue. It occurred to me if I painted my rocker blue, I might want to paint my planter boxes blue as well."

"I have some swatches you can take if you want to pick out a shade. Or, if you have a specific color in mind, I can mix pretty much anything you want."

I took one of the hard candies Hap kept on the counter, unwrapped it, and popped it in my mouth. "Thanks. I'll just take some swatches for now. I'm supposed to meet Brady at the lake after work, so I shouldn't dawdle."

"Heard he was trying to train a couple of pups for Jimmy Early."

I nodded. "Brothers Brady wants to place together. Jimmy seems interested in taking them, but he needs them to be able to swim."

"Makes sense. Jimmy spends a good part of his life on the water." Hap picked up his mail and began tossing the flyers in the garbage. "Spoke to Hattie over the weekend. She said you and Bree are trying to find Chip Townsend."

I adjusted my mailbag on my shoulder. "We are. Do you know anything that might help?"

"I might." Hap set the mail back on the counter. "He used to work for me when he lived here.

Sweeping up, mostly. He was always looking to make a few bucks, and I was happy to have the help."

"I didn't realize that. Hattie didn't mention it."

"Don't think she knew. It was an informal arrangement. He'd come by when he needed money, and if I had chores, I'd let him do them."

Suddenly, I slipped my bag back off my shoulder again and set it at my feet. It looked like I was going to be there for a while after all. "Did you talk much when he was working for you?"

"Some. Chip wasn't the sort to overshare, but we'd tip back a cold one from time to time and chat."

"A cold one? You had a beer with him?"

"Coke."

"Oh, that makes more sense. Go on. What did you talk about?"

"This and that. Fishing, mostly. Chip didn't always get on all that well with the other kids in school, but he loved to go fishing."

I didn't see how this would help me, but Hap liked to take the long way around when making a point, so I'd play along. "And do you think fishing is important to finding him?"

"Talked to Tony. He came by for some supplies for one of the projects he's working on. He mentioned you'd been searching databases like the DMV, looking for a record of where Chip might have lived in the past quarter century."

"That's true, but what does that have to do with fishing?"

"Nothing. Exactly. But talking about a driver's license got me thinking of fishing licenses. When Chip lived here, he went fishing as often as he could.

Seems to me if he's going to be in town, he might be looking to visit a few of his old haunts."

"And he'd need a fishing license." I finally caught on.

"Exactly. Might look into someone by the name of Greg Townsend applying for one."

I smiled. "Thanks, Hap. That's a very good idea."

I left the store and crossed the street, making a beeline for Mike's office. I'd wanted to speak to him anyway, but as long as I had Hap's suggestion fresh in my mind, I figured I may as well do some crisscrossing of my regular route and speak to him now rather than later in the day. When Tilly and I entered the reception area, where Frank normally sat, we found Mike leaning against the counter, talking on the phone. I motioned that I needed to speak to him and he raised a finger, letting me know he'd be a minute. Frank must be off today, or just out on a call, because his desk chair was empty.

I took a seat there while I waited for Mike. Tilly stretched out on the floor next to me, and I reached into my bag and drew out one of the doggy treats I always carried. She politely accepted it and then settled down to enjoy her midmorning snack.

"You're here early," Mike said after he got off the phone and turned his attention to me.

"I was at Hap's and he brought up something I wanted you to check out for me."

"You know I'm not your private PI, right?"

I shrugged. "I know, but this is important. Hap and I got to chatting about Chip Townsend, and he told me that Chip loved to fish when he lived here. It's been such great weather, we figured if he planned to be in town for more than just the one day, he might decide to visit some of his old fishing holes. I hoped you could check to see if he's applied for a fishing license. If not yet, maybe you can keep an eye out to see if he applies for one later in the week, or even next week, if we haven't found him by then."

"Seems like a long shot."

I lifted a shoulder. "Yeah, it is. But I'll take any lead I can get. I don't suppose you were able to track down either Edna's emergency contact, Beth Wright, or her next of kin?"

"I did find Beth Wright. She passed away a year ago. As for a next of kin, no one was ever identified. Edna left burial instructions, asking to be cremated and then buried in a small plot in Kalispell, which she'd already paid for. She also asked that any money she had at her time of death be donated to the assisted-living facility where she spent her final days. She didn't have a lot. A few hundred bucks."

"Dang. I guess both those leads are dead ends."

"Maybe, but I found something else. When I called the assisted-living facility to verify that Edna's final requests were honored, they told me that they had a box of her things. They were personal in nature: receipts, financial records, photos. They didn't want to simply throw them away, but they didn't know who to send them to. I told the woman I spoke to that I was trying to track down her son and would accept possession of them. Frank's picking up the box right now. I'm hoping there might be a clue somewhere in the photos. Frank should be back within the half hour, if you want to come back by."

I looked at the clock. "I need to make up some time with my deliveries, but my lunch is scheduled for an hour from now. I'll be back then." I got up and slung my bag over my shoulder. "Thanks, Mike. It means a lot that you're pitching in the way you have."

"Like I said before, notifying next of kin of the death of a loved one is part of my job."

"Maybe, but Edna didn't die in White Eagle, so technically, it isn't your job. Either way, I appreciate it."

I tried to make as many deliveries as possible in the next hour, keeping my head down and avoiding eye contact as I dropped off each merchant's mail, attempting to avoid any attempt at chitchat. The few people who weren't busy when I stopped in and tried to start up conversations were quickly and politely shut down with a comment that I was way behind schedule and needed to put the pedal to the metal if I was going to finish all my deliveries by the end of the day. The two businesses where I knew I wouldn't get away with a drop and run were Bree's bookstore and Mom and Aunt Ruthie's café. I wanted to have the full hour with Mike if I needed it, so I bypassed their places with the intention of catching them at the end of the day.

When I returned to the police station, I found Mike talking with Frank. The counter was littered with items they seemed to have separated into piles based, I assumed, on content. "Did you find anything?"

"Maybe," Mike answered. "Edna's bank statements indicate she lived from Social Security check to Social Security check, as we'd suspected, and most of the other documents and receipts seem pretty routine. We still need to analyze the photos, but there's one receipt that might be of interest."

I set my mailbag on the floor next to where Tilly sat, waiting for an invitation by either Frank or Mike for a proper hello. "And what is that?"

"A receipt for a storage unit. It looks like Edna had the unit for about a decade and paid the rent annually. The unit is paid for through August, so we're hoping whatever she left in it is still there."

"Can we check it out?"

"I made a few phone calls and got the go-ahead to take a peek. The unit is just north of town. I'm heading there now. Do you want to come?"

"Heck yeah." I glanced at Tilly. "Can Tilly ride along in your car?"

Mike shrugged. "Sure. As long as she's willing to ride in the back."

I glanced at Frank. "Can I leave my mailbag here?"

"Just toss it under my desk. No one will bother it. Tilly can wait here with me if you want as well."

"What if you get a call?"

"I'll put her in Mike's office and call you. The station will be locked up and you'll only be about ten minutes away. She'd be fine."

I glanced at Tilly. She loved to hang out with Frank, and I wasn't sure what we'd find in the storage unit. "Okay. Hopefully, we won't be long."

I explained to Tilly that she was going to hang out with Frank for a few minutes while I went to check something out, then followed Mike to his squad car.

"So, how was your fishing trip?" I asked as we headed to the storage facility.

"It was fun. I didn't catch any fish, but Bree caught one. Her first, if you can believe it."

My mouth fell open. "Bree went fishing with you?"

Mike nodded. "I mentioned I planned to go up to that little lake at the base of the National Park when I was at her place on Saturday, helping her replace the part of her fence that was damaged over the winter. She said she'd never been fishing and didn't think it would be her cup of tea, but I managed to convince her that the peace and solitude of backcountry fishing was something to experience, so she gave it a try."

I was stunned. Really stunned. Bree was my best friend and I loved her, but we were very different. She was polished and sophisticated, with little tolerance for dirt or clutter, and both her home and her bookstore were always immaculate. She could be talked into a hike every now and then, but fishing?

"And she actually fished? She didn't just sit and watch you?"

Mike laughed. "She actually fished. Like I said, she even caught one. She was close to hysterical when I explained that we'd need to kill it before we could eat it, so I threw it back. I don't think she's going to run out and buy a bunch of fishing gear, but she admitted the experience was pleasant overall."

Well I'll be. Bree and Mike. I knew they'd gone out to dinner on Friday, but I'd had no idea that would lead to them spending the entire weekend together. I wasn't sure how I felt about that. They'd been lifelong friends, and I supposed everything they'd done would fall into the friend category, but what if it didn't? What if they were heading toward something more? I realized I should talk to Bree and get her spin on things. I wanted Bree to find a great guy like Mike, and I wanted Mike to find a great woman like Bree, but I wasn't sure I wanted them to find each other.

When we arrived at the storage unit, we found it packed from top to bottom. There were boxes labeled and sealed, quite a bit of furniture, which may have been unsold inventory from when Edna closed her antique store, and other miscellaneous items.

"There's no way we have time to go through this right now," I said to Mike.

"Yeah. There's a lot more than I anticipated. We'll need to come back."

"I'm meeting Brady at the lake at six to help with some dog training. I should be done by eight, if you don't mind meeting me here then." I pointed toward the ceiling. "The unit has an overhead light."

"I'll check with the owner, find out what time they lock the front gate. If it looks like we'll have enough time to make it worth the trip, I'm fine to come back tonight. I'll text you later."

I let my eyes dart around the contents of the large room. "Edna might not have had cash when she died, but all these antiques must be worth a pretty penny. It seems to me there's another reason to track down Chip Townsend. If Edna didn't leave the items in this room to anyone specifically, chances are all of this belongs to him."

Mike took me back to town, where I collected Tilly and my mailbag. I managed to get the rest of my route done in record time until I reached the bookstore. Luckily, I still had an hour before I had to meet Brady. Bree had been my last drop-off by design, so I had plenty of time to try to figure out what was going on between my brother and my best friend.

Chapter 11

Bree was just locking up for the day when I arrived, and she waved at me through the glass door, turned the key in the lock, and ushered me inside. Then she relocked the door and turned the "Open" sign to "Closed."

"I'd all but given up on you today," Bree said as I handed her the stack of mail I'd been holding back for her.

"It's been a busy day. I've had a lot of deliveries, plus I spent some time with Mike trying to track down Chip Townsend."

"Any luck?" Bree asked as she began closing out the cash register.

"Maybe. When I dropped off Hap's mail, he mentioned Chip liked to fish," I said, explaining how they'd gotten to know each other. "I thought it might be worthwhile to check in to fishing licenses."

Bree scrunched up her nose. "I can unequivocally state that fishing isn't as peaceful and serene as some men make it out to be." She tilted her head, looking in my direction, a fistful of twenty-dollar bills in her hand. "Do you know that the expectation is not only that you catch the fish, fighting off mosquitos and other flying insects all the while, but once you've caught it you have to kill and clean it?"

"Mike said he took you out for your maiden voyage."

Bree's face wore a look of disgust. "He tricked me is what he did. He waited until I was in a pliant and malleable mood and tricked me."

"Pliant and malleable?" I suppressed a chuckle.

Bree quickly counted the pile of money in her hand, recorded the amount in her ledger, placed it in a bank bag, and picked up the next pile of bills, tens, from the register. "He called me on Friday, not long after you left, and told me that you'd been by to ask about Chip. He said you'd mentioned I'd wanted to go out for dinner but you had been busy, so he suggested the two of us go together. I was in the mood to do something more festive than laundry, so I agreed. We went to that new Mexican place in Kalispell."

"Kalispell? That seems like a long drive for dinner."

"Not really. It was a nice night and Mike suggested we take his Harley. It seemed like a good distraction from the mundane life I've settled into, so I agreed. We had a wonderful time."

Bree on a Harley? Perhaps I didn't know her as well as I thought.

"Anyway," Bree continued, "during dinner I mentioned that part of my fence had been destroyed over the winter and needed to be replaced. I asked him if he knew any handymen who would do a good job for a fair price. Mike said he was totally free on Saturday and would come over to fix it for me. I offered to pay him, but he refused. He said I could make him dinner in exchange for the labor. You know the spring is my slowest time and I need to watch my expenses, so I agreed. He came over in the morning, made a list of what he'd need, used his truck to go get the wood, then had the fence not only repaired but painted by five. He barbecued steaks, and I put some Idahos and corn on the cob on the grill." Bree smiled. "It was actually very nice. I know Mike can be a tool at times, but it was very sweet of him to spend his entire Saturday fixing my fence."

I lifted a shoulder. "He can be a good guy when he gets it in his mind to be. So how did all that lead to fishing?"

Bree placed the ten-dollar bills in the bank bag and started on the fives. "While we were relaxing on my deck, enjoying the beautiful day, sipping wine, and relaxing, Mike told me that he was going fishing on Sunday. He asked me if I wanted to go, and I, of course, immediately said no. But then he started to paint the picture of an isolated lake in the middle of the forest with an old wooden deck on one end that someone had built decades ago. He talked about lounging in the sun with a cold beer as we soaked up some rays. It sounded nice. Serene. It was probably the wine, but before I knew what had hit me, I found myself agreeing to go."

I laughed out loud.

"It isn't funny."

"I take it Mike oversold the experience?"

Bree nodded. "I'll admit it was fun at first. I wore my bikini, laid out in the sun, and read a book while he fished. After I'd had enough sun we moved to a shady spot. Mike had brought an extra fishing pole and asked if I wanted to try. I really didn't, but he convinced me that casting the line, slowly reeling it in, and then casting it again, was an almost Zenlike experience. I was bored by then, so I gave it a go. And it was fun. At first. But then I caught that dang-blasted fish, and everything went downhill from there."

I put my hand on Bree's arm as she picked up the pile of ones still left in the cash register. "I'm sorry Mike tricked you. He should have known you and fishing weren't a good mix. I guess it was partly my fault for suggesting he ask you to dinner on Friday."

"It wasn't your fault. I had the best time on Friday night I'd had in a very long time. And I got my fence fixed for the cost of a meal. Less than the cost of a meal, because Mike bought the steaks. And Sunday wasn't all that bad except for the fish. If I go again, I'll be fishing without a hook."

I raised a brow. "If you go again? Are you thinking of going again?"

Bree shrugged. "I don't have definite plans, but it was a nice day when you take the fish out of the equation. So maybe. How about you? How was your weekend? Did Shaggy mind his manners on Friday, or did he act like a toddler the way he usually does?"

"Shaggy didn't show, so it was just Tony and me. And it was fun. We played the game he had to test and on Saturday I helped him build some garden boxes for his deck. We even planted some herbs."

Bree tilted her head. "Sounds very domestic."

I smiled. "I guess it was. I forget there's more to Tony than the computer stuff. He likes to cook. He learned from his grandmother in Italy."

It was Bree's turn to look surprised. "Really? All I've ever seen him eat is takeout and frozen pizza."

"I think that has more to do with being busy than anything else." I looked at the clock. "Geez, I have to go. I'm meeting Brady for some dog training."

"Want to grab dinner after?"

"Actually, Brady mentioned bringing a picnic. We're working with the terrier brothers at the beach. And after that I'm meeting Mike at the storage facility north of town."

"Storage facility?"

I quickly explained Edna's storage room, then hurried off to meet Brady.

******

Brady, Jagger, and Bowie were waiting for Tilly and me when we arrived. By the look of things, Brady had been working on some basic commands while he waited but wisely released the boys to relax when he saw my Jeep approaching. The odds of them maintaining a sit/stay once they realized Tilly and I had come to play was slim to none, and in the early stages of training it was best to avoid situations where a dog would be unsuccessful.

Brady held on to both dogs' collars until I'd come to a complete stop. Once I was out of the Jeep and had opened the door for Tilly, Brady let them go. The three dogs greeted one another with wiggles and wagging tails accentuated by yips of happiness. I loved it when dogs came together in greeting. Their capacity for unbridled joy was beautiful to see.

"Right on time," Brady said as I walked over and gave him a quick hug.

"Have you been here long?"

"About fifteen minutes. I used the time to work on a few basics with the brothers. They're really coming along. Today is the first time I've really been able to get them to focus on me with both together."

"Maybe it's the change of scenery that did it." I looked around at the lake, beach, and forest in the distance. "There's a lot to take in. The location could have been even more distracting than the training room at the shelter, but it also might be somewhat overwhelming, even though we were here on Saturday. The boys probably didn't get out a lot with their former owner. They know you. Trust you. They most likely look to you for direction in this new and initially uncomfortable situation."

"Yeah. I guess." He glanced at the brothers, who looked as if they might wiggle out of their skin with excitement now that Tilly was here. "Are you ready?"

I slipped off my tennis shoes, opened my bag, and grabbed three balls. "As I'll ever be."

I called all three dogs and told them to sit. Then, as I drew back my arm to throw the first of the balls, I yelled for them to fetch. Tilly took off like a dart, though the brothers looked less sure. I tossed the second ball into the water and yelled fetch again. Jagger hesitated just a bit, then went in after it. I hadn't tossed it far, so he didn't need to swim; I figured it was best to start slowly. I held the third ball in front of Bowie's face. "Do you want it?" He locked his eyes on the ball and jumped up on his hind legs. I tossed it in the water, even closer to the shore than the one I'd tossed for Jagger. "Okay, fetch."

It took a good thirty minutes of playing with the dogs, wading out farther and farther as we did so, before the brothers were faced with the choice to either swim out to where Brady and I were playing with Tilly or watch from afar. Both dogs barked and pranced and eventually Jagger's excitement got the better of him. Before I knew it, he was swimming directly to me. "Good boy, Jagger. Way to swim. Just a little farther." I held out my arms to him. Committed now that he could no longer stand, he headed directly to me. As soon as he reached me, I lifted him into my arms and rewarded him with hugs and kisses. Then I walked him back to the shore and we repeated the game several times. Jagger seemed to enjoy paddling around in the water once he figured out he wasn't going to sink, but it took most of the evening to get Bowie to try it for the first time. We didn't want to stop until Bowie had a chance to repeat the behavior several times, so it was already seven-thirty by the time we called it a day.

"I brought food," Brady said.

I glanced at my watch. "That sounds so good, but I'm supposed to meet Mike at eight." I took a few minutes to explain our search for Chip and Edna's storage shed.

"Wow. I hope you find the guy, and I totally understand. Tomorrow?"

"I have plans tomorrow, but now that the boys are used to the water and seem to enjoy swimming, I think they'll swim for you even without Tilly as enticement. Maybe one of the other volunteers can come with you tomorrow. If it doesn't work out and you feel like you still need Tilly, we can come out on Wednesday."

"Book club is Wednesday."

I cringed. Brady was a lot better about making it to the book club Bree held on Wednesday evenings than I was. "Okay then, Thursday." I ran a towel over Tilly once I'd dried my own legs and pulled on my shorts. "Or better yet, have Jimmy come help you with the boys. You may as well find out sooner rather than later if there's chemistry there."

Brady nodded. "I'll call him when I get home. Are you still on for speed dating on Saturday?"

"Wouldn't miss it. If I don't talk to you before, I'll see you then."

I grabbed a granola bar from my glove box before I started the Jeep and headed back toward town. It looked like I wasn't going to get dinner and I was starving, but I didn't have time to stop to grab a bite to eat. Mike was already there when Tilly and I arrived at the storage facility and, much to my surprise, so was Bree.

"I didn't expect you to be here," I greeted her.

"Your story intrigued me, so I called Mike and asked if he minded if I tagged along. We knew you were training with Brady, so we went ahead and got started. I'm not an expert, but I know a bit about antiques and I can tell you, there's a lot of really valuable stuff in here."

It just looked like a lot of old furniture to me, but what did I know? "Did you find anything that might help us track Chip down?"

"Not yet," Mike said. "But we've just started. It looks like the stuff toward the back is inventory from the antique store. The boxes and smaller items closer to the front appear to be personal items, most likely stored when she moved from her house to the assisted-living facility."

"I found a box of photos," Bree volunteered. "I've been sorting through them, hoping we'll find a clue to where the special place Chip referred to in the card might be."

I looked at Mike. "Are we totally certain Edna only had one child? Maybe she had another one who was older and never lived here?"

"I ran a search. The only birth record I could find with Edna's name on it was for Greg Fairchild, who was born in Chicago in 1973."

"The card was postmarked from Chicago," I volunteered.

"It looked as if Edna Townsend married Dorian Fairchild in July 1970 in a civil ceremony in Chicago," Mike informed me. "Greg was born on June 18, 1973, and Fairchild, who worked as a long-haul trucker, was convicted of killing six women along his route in 1987."

I felt a shiver crawl up my spine. The fact that this serial killer was a long haul trucker the same as my father had hit a bit too close to home. I couldn't help but wonder if the reason my own father had disappeared wasn't equally as disturbing. I was tempted to fill Mike in on the whole confusing mystery but realized that would be rash at this point so I didn't.

Mike continued. "Greg had his last name changed legally to Townsend six months after his father's conviction, and Greg and Edna moved to White Eagle in January of 1988. Greg was kicked out of school in January of 1991 and left town in 1993 or '94. I couldn't find anything that indicated a specific date for his departure."

I paused and leaned a hip against an old hutch. "So, if Greg started off in Chicago and then sent the letter from Chicago approximately twenty-five years later, maybe he's moved back there. Are you sure there isn't any evidence of someone named Greg Townsend living in Chicago or thereabouts?"

Mike shook his head. "Nothing. He may have changed his name again after he fell out with his mother. The name Townsend still linked him to his father in a roundabout way because it was his mother's maiden name."

"Tony said the same thing." I stepped away from the hutch and looked around the room. There were a lot of things there. If there was a clue to be found, how on earth would we be able to discriminate between the relevant and the nonrelevant?

Mike made his way toward the back of the room while Bree continued to sift through the box she'd been looking in. "I think I found something," she announced, holding up a photo.

I walked to her and she handed it to me. It was of a young boy who looked to be around ten, standing in front of a building made of wood, old and in need of maintenance, though he had a huge grin on his face. "Why do you think this is significant?" I asked.

Bree handed me a stack of photos. "Because there are six other photos of the same boy in front of the same building. It looks like maybe one a year for six years or thereabouts, based on the last photo, where he looks to be well into his teens."

"I see what you're getting at. If the boy in the photo is Chip—and I assume it is—this building was a place he and the photographer, who for now I'll say is Edna, visited on multiple occasions. If they chose this as a place for an annual photograph, we can assume it was special to them." I looked at the photos more closely. "I wonder where it is. The building doesn't look familiar, but the background does. It could have been taken somewhere in the mountains."

"Maybe Edna and her son visited this area when they lived in Chicago. Maybe that's the reason they chose to move here when Chip's father was convicted; they'd visited before and liked it," Bree suggested.

Mike took the stack of photos and began to sort through them. "I'm not sure I know exactly what building it is offhand, but I sort of feel as if I've seen it before. Maybe it's in the park."

I knew Mike was referring to nearby Glacier National Park.

"There are quite a few cabins in that area, as well as in the village, and there are other park buildings," I agreed.

He put one of the photos in his pocket. "I'll send a copy of this to the park service. Maybe someone who works in the area will recognize the structure."

I picked up the box Bree had been sorting through. "I'll take this box home with me and go through it some more. Maybe something else will pop. Right now, I'm going to go home and grab something to eat. I haven't had more than a granola bar all day."

Chapter 12

Tuesday, May 8

I'd spent hours looking through Edna's photos, resulting in serious sleep deprivation and making the day seem endless despite the continuation of our beautiful spring weather. I hadn't found anything in the box I would necessarily consider to be relevant, though I'd found a wedding photo of Edna with a tall, dark-haired man with small eyes and an emotionless stare. He, I decided, looked exactly like a serial killer. Even then. I guess I'd been operating under the assumption that Dorian Fairchild was a regular guy when Edna married him. At least on the outside. Given his intense stare and stony expression as he posed for a photo with the woman he'd chosen to spend his life with, I couldn't imagine what had motivated Edna to marry him in the first place.

The only other item that seemed at all significant in the box was a heart-shaped locket with a photo of a baby inside. I assumed it was Chip. Mike was going to follow up with the photos of the building, and when I saw Tony tonight, I planned to give him the most recent photo we'd found of Chip and ask him to use his facial recognition software to try to find a photo of modern-day Chip.

"Afternoon, Frank," I called out to my brother's partner on entering the police station. I tossed a pile of mail on his desk. "Is Mike in his office?"

"He's out on a call. I'm guessing he should be back shortly. Can I help you with anything?"

I sat on the corner of his desk. "No. I just figured that as long as I was stopping by to drop off the mail, I'd see if he'd had any luck locating the building in the photos we found."

"I know he sent it to the local forest service office and the administration office for the National Park Service. As far as I know, he hasn't gotten a bite; as least not as of when he left. I looked at the photo myself. If you ask me, the building the kid is standing in front of is one of those old forest service cabins off Highway 2."

"Yeah, I had the same thought. If it's a cabin and not a commercial building, it's going to be hard to find. There are a lot of cabins dotted along the highway. It would be impossible to find a particular cabin with the limited view provided by the photo."

Frank frowned. "And how do you think identifying the building is going to help you locate Chip?"

I slipped my bag off my shoulder and onto the floor, near where Tilly was sitting, waiting patiently.

"I don't think it will help us find him, but if we don't find him, trying to figure out where he'll be at noon on Sunday may be the only shot we have at letting him know of his mother's death."

"Seems odd he doesn't already know."

I shrugged. "Maybe. But if the two hadn't been in touch, he might not have heard. Mike and Tony both think he may have been out of the country. He might have returned just recently. That would explain why they can't find either work records or a driver's license."

"I guess that makes sense." Frank looked at the photo again. "You show this to Hap?"

"Not yet, but I will. Hap likes to fish, and he said Chip did too. Maybe the cabin in the photo is a place the two chatted about when Chip worked for Hap as a teenager." I stood and slipped on my bag. "Let Mike know I was here. Tell him to call me if he hears anything."

"Will do. Enjoy the nice day."

I looked out the window at the blue sky and snowcapped mountains in the distance. "I'll do that. You have a nice day too."

The next few hours passed quickly. It seemed a lot of folks were out and about today, which meant that most of the merchants I delivered to were busy with customers and therefore didn't have time to chat. I even managed to get in and out of Bree's place without more than a wave, which was rare even when she was busy. By the time I reached Hap's it was close to three, which was excellent, because I'd done my route in a backward loop, which meant he was the last of my deliveries. It would be nice to finish early and get home. Tony was coming over to install my planter boxes.

"Wondered what happened to you today," Hap said when Tilly and I came in and I dropped a pile of mail on his counter.

"Changed things up a bit."

"Been doing that quite a bit lately. I suppose I'd get bored doing the same thing every day myself. Did you settle on a color for your rocker?"

I nodded and handed him the sample card for the shade of blue I'd selected. "I had Mike pick up the rocker and bring it to my cabin this morning. I can't wait to get started. How much paint do you think I'll need?"

Hap twisted his lips. "Are you planning on painting the planter boxes the same color?"

"I'm thinking about it. It occurred to me that painting the boxes a darker blue than the chair might provide a nice contrast."

Hap handed me a medium-sized can. "I'd start with this. It should be plenty for the chair. If you decide on the same color for the garden boxes, I can mix up more. If you decide to go with a different shade, you won't have purchased more of this blue than you need."

I smiled. "Okay, thanks. I can't wait to get started."

"I have some outgoing mail for you." Hap reached under the counter, then set a stack of envelopes secured with a rubber band in front of me. I picked it up and put it in my bag.

"Before I go," I took one of the photos of Chip in front of the wooden building from the pocket of my bag, "will you look at this?" I passed it to Hap.

He gave it a brief look. "Looks like a young Chip. Did you track him down?"

I shook my head. "Not yet. We found a bunch of photos of him standing in front of this building. Based on my best guess, the photos, six in all, span the years between Chip being eight or nine and maybe thirteen or fourteen. Do you recognize the building?"

Hap took a moment to really look at the photo. "Seems familiar." He narrowed his gaze, then pointed to an object off to the side that was too blurry to really make out. "If this here is a gas pump, I'd say this is the old filling station out on the highway."

I took a closer look at the blurry object. There was no way to know what it was from the angle of this photo. I pulled the other photos out of my bag, but the angle was the same on all of them.

"Seems odd that Edna, or someone, would take a photo of Chip in front of an old filling station," I said.

"Maybe. But the one I'm thinking of is the last station before you turn up the dirt road to the seasonal cabins. There's a good fishing lake up that road. Most who rent the seasonal cabins get their gas and supplies there. You can't tell by the photos you have, but if my assumption is correct, the building Chip is standing in front of is a camp store. They carry a few grocery items, propane, firewood, that sort of thing."

"Is it still in business?"

Hap lifted a shoulder. "I haven't been up that way in quite a while, but it was still there the last time I checked."

"How far is it from here?"

"I guess forty or fifty minutes." Hap turned and pulled a map from a display behind him and opened it up on the counter. He smoothed it with his hands and pointed to a spot just off the highway. "The filling station I'm thinking of is right about here." He ran a finger up a thin line. "This here is the dirt road up to the cabins." He pointed to a small lake. "And this here is the lake I mentioned." Hap looked up from the map. "It might not hurt to take a drive out there. If it's the right place, you should be able to match the photos up with the building."

"Thanks. I will. Can I buy that map?"

Hap folded it up and handed it to me. "Consider it a gift."

By the time I walked back to my Jeep, drove to the post office, dropped off my bag, and drove home, it was after four, but still early compared to most days. I wasn't expecting to see Tony quite this early, but his truck was in the drive when I pulled up. Tilly began wagging her tail, the tip hitting the door next to her and the can of paint on the seat between us alternately, and Titan ran around the house from the back. I grabbed the paint and the map, opened the driver's side door, slid out, motioned for Tilly to hop out the same door, and then bent down to greet Titan.

"Hey, sweetie," I said as I vigorously rubbed the shepherd in greeting. "Where's your daddy?"

Titan didn't answer, but the sound of hammering coming from the back deck gave me the answer I needed.

Titan and Tilly followed me around the house, where I found a shirtless Tony, slick with sweat, hammering two boards together. I waited until he was done with the nail he was working on, then greeted him.

He looked up, surprise evident on his face. He put down his hammer and grabbed a T-shirt from the railing, and quickly pulled it over his head. "I didn't know you'd be here this early."

"I'm usually not home until after five, but I finished early today." I noticed Tang and Tinder sitting on a lounge chair out of the corner of my eye. "The garden boxes look perfect. Exactly what I imagined."

Tony wiped the sweat from his brow with the back of his arm. "I worked the design out in my head. I think they're going to add a lot to your outdoor space." Tony glanced at the paint in my hands. "I think you're going to need more paint."

"This is for my rocking chair. I'm thinking of using a darker blue for the garden boxes."

Tony placed the next board to be hammered in place. "I saw the old rocker on your front porch. Looks like you found a sturdy one."

"It's exactly what I've been looking for. I can't wait to get started on the painting, but first I have something to show you." I held up the map. "If you want to take a break, I have beer and cola in the refrigerator, and I can show you what I found out today."

Tony tossed his hammer onto a chair. "I could use a break, and a cola sounds good."

In the cabin, I grabbed two colas from the refrigerator, then showed Tony the photos with the wooden building in the background and the place on the map Hap had pointed out to me, then asked if he thought it would be worth our while to drive out to the old gas station and take a look around. Even if we could determine the building in the photos and the food-and-gas stop Hap remembered were one and the same, it didn't guarantee anyone would remember Chip or know how to contact him today, but it was something to do, and I felt like we were running into dead end after dead end.

Tony said he could plug the most recent photo of Chip into his facial recognition program. It was unlikely he'd get a hit, but it certainly couldn't hurt. He wanted to take a quick shower and change into clean clothes before making the trip, so I ran upstairs and changed out of my uniform while he put his tools away. He'd come back tomorrow to finish up, so he left everything in my mudroom.

I fed the kittens and grabbed food to bring along for the dogs. I'd feed Tilly at Tony's while he showered and changed. We'd bring the dogs with us; they'd enjoy the ride and we weren't going all that far.

When I glanced at my unpainted chair sitting on the front deck I felt a twinge of indecision. I really wanted to get it painted, but it wasn't urgent, and finding Chip before he made the trip to White Eagle from wherever he was seemed a lot more important.

******

When Tony came down from showering and changing his clothes, we went down to the basement. He scanned the photo of Chip into his computer, then typed in some commands to activate the facial recognition program. The blinking lights and whir of the equipment made me think of other mysteries Tony was looking in to for me.

"Any news about Luciana Parisi's murder?" I asked.

"I haven't found anything, although to be honest, I haven't put a ton of time into it, but my contact did shoot me a message. Apparently, the investigator has a new lead. He either didn't know or didn't say what it was, but based on his tone, I wouldn't be surprised if there isn't an arrest relating to the murder in the upcoming weeks."

"That's great. If they identify and apprehend the guilty party, that eliminates the need for us to worry about it one way or the other. I'm just glad my mom isn't talking about making a trip to Italy until summer. I know the case has been open for seven years, but if the investigator does have a lead, hopefully things will be wrapped up long before that, or Romero finds an opportunity to make another trip here."

Tony pounded out a few more commands, then stood up. "Okay, that should do it. It's a long shot. A very long shot. But it's worth a try. Are you ready to roll?"

I nodded. "I'm also starving. Let's grab a burger after we check out the tourist stop Hap told me about. A big one." My mouth began to water. "With fries."

Chapter 13

The trip out of town to the sparsely populated area dotted with hiking trails, clearwater lakes, and small seasonal cabins, was uneventful. The dogs sat happily in the backseat of Tony's truck with tongues lolling to the side as the wind from the open windows caressed their faces. The rivers, creeks, and streams that ran under the highway were swollen with spring runoff, creating overflow along the uncrowded highway where water spilled from the barriers. Tony slowed and eased past the slow-moving channels of water as we made our way farther into the dense forest that coated the area with thick groves of dark green pines entangled with delicate, quaking aspens that turned the area a bright yellow in the fall.

"It's been a while since I've been up this way," Tony commented as the road meandered along and we enjoyed the spring evening, while rock tunes blared on the stereo.

"For me as well." As we wound our way through a narrow canyon, I looked out the window at the rocky crags that lined the sides of the road. "I intended to take a drive out this way last October, but life got busy and I never made it."

"We'll make a point to come together this fall. Maybe bring a picnic."

I leaned my head back and relaxed into the breeze from the open window. "That'd be nice. There's this one spot at the end of an old logging road where I especially like to go when the leaves turn."

"Sawmill Pond."

I sat forward. "You know the area. All those aspens tangled up with the fern and vine maple. Simply breathtaking. And most years that little stream trickles down over the craggy bluff at the far side of the pond, creating the most beautiful waterfall you're ever likely to see. I keep thinking I'll snap a photo of it to hang on my wall, but I never seem to remember to do it once I'm there."

The song we'd been listening to segued to a classic from the sixties, and Tony and I both sang along. After the song wrapped up, Tony spoke. "According to the map Hap gave you, the filling station and store should be just up ahead on the right."

"There." I pointed to a sign in the distance.

The small oasis was a one-stop shopping mecca for the campers, fishermen, and hunters who frequented the area. Toward the center of the large flat lot was a four-pump gas station that had been refurbished in the past decade by the look of things. Beyond that was a medium-sized log building that appeared to serve as a general store. To the right of that was a small diner, to the left a laundromat. Tony parked off to the side, out of the way.

We instructed the dogs to stay, got out, and headed to the little store. I loved everything about it. It was quaint, and charming, and made me think of warm summer nights spent telling ghost stories around a campfire. The s'mores display had my mouth watering and the water toys made me yearn for the simple, carefree summers of my childhood.

The clutter of a country theme mixed with mountain accents was not only charming but appeared to be functional as well. The center of the store, closest to the cash register, housed food items including canned and boxed goods, baking supplies, bread, and a variety of candy, chips, and other junk food. There was an area in the back to the right that displayed fishing gear and supplies, camping equipment, flashlights, cookstoves, and pretty much anything a camper or fisherman might want. And all the way to the left, souvenirs, sweatshirts, T-shirts, and other bric-a-brac folks tend to buy while on vacation were neatly arranged.

"Can I help you folks?" asked a short, portly man wearing old-fashioned denim overalls over a red-and-black-flannel shirt.

I approached with a smile. "Hi. My name is Tess." I nodded to my right. "And this is Tony. We're looking for someone who has worked here for a long time and might remember a visitor from years back."

"How long?"

"About thirty years."

The man tilted his head to one side. "You'll want to speak to Turk. He's owned the place for the past fifty years."

"Do you know where we can find him?"

The man used his thumb to point toward the hallway behind him.

"He's here?" I clarified.

"In his office. Second door on the right."

I thanked him, and Tony and I headed to the back of the building. The door to the office was open. A tall man with a thin frame was sitting at a desk growling at a ledger. Whatever he was looking at seemed to be making him more than just a little angry.

"Turk?" I said in a small voice, hoping my inquiry wouldn't be met with the same growl.

He looked up at me with a frown. His momentary confusion gave way to a softening. "Can I help you?"

I gave him our names, then said, "We wanted to ask you if you remembered this boy." I handed him the most recent photo we had of Chip.

He took a moment to look and then looked up and stared into my eyes. "You said you were a friend of Greg's?"

I shook my head. "No, not a friend. But we do have something of his we'd like to return. We have news for him as well. News about his mother. We found some photos and realized he must have spent quite a bit of time here as a child. We hoped someone would remember him and would be able to tell us how we could reach him."

Turk glanced at Tony with blue eyes faded with age. He slowly looked him up and down, then returned his gaze to me. "Perhaps you should tell me exactly what it is you have for Greg."

I took a step farther into the office and handed him the Mother's Day card Bree had received. I explained that, based on the note, Edna's son didn't know she had passed. I assured Turk that we only wanted to inform him of his mother's death and prevent him from making a trip to his special place for nothing.

Turk bowed his head of snowy hair. "I'm sorry to hear about Edna. She was a nice woman. Brought her young'un here every summer until her husband was arrested. Never saw her again after that."

"So, the photo I showed you must have been taken when Greg was a freshman in high school."

Turk nodded. "Sounds about right."

"We know Edna moved to White Eagle after her husband was sent to prison. She lived there until she moved to an assisted-living facility in Kalispell a couple of years ago. She passed away about six months ago. As far as I can tell, the local police never tracked down her next of kin. I don't suppose you have any idea how we can reach her son?"

He shook his head. "Sorry. It's been a lot of years." He looked down at the card he still held. "I have an idea about the special place, though."

"Really? Where?"

He stood up straight and tall, despite his age. "Come with me. I'll show you."

Tony and I followed him out of the building toward a groomed path marked with timbers. The trail, damp but not muddy, wound through tall trees and lush undergrowth made up of ferns, moss, vine maples, dogwood, and other shade-loving trees and shrubs. After we'd walked a half mile or so, the trail opened onto a large meadow papered with brightly colored wildflowers. In the center was a large pond that was home to a variety of birds, mainly, at first glance, Canada geese and wild ducks.

"It's beautiful," I gasped in pure delight.

"There." He pointed. To the left of the pond, under a flowering dogwood, was a wooden bench. He left the trail and walked across the rough terrain toward the lovely seating area. When we came to the bench, he pointed to words carved into the seat. *To Mama love Greggy*

"I helped Greg make this for his mama when he was maybe ten or eleven. They'd come up for the summer, like they always did, but Edna had something heavy on her mind. She never said what was bothering her, but she wasn't her usual bubbly self. She seemed tired and weak, like she hadn't been eating and sleeping right."

"You knew them well?" I asked

He shrugged. "As well as can be. Every summer for quite a few years, Edna and Greg rented a cabin just up the road from my property. Most every day they'd stop at the diner, order a boxed lunch, then come over to this little pond to fish and swim."

"And Greg's father?"

He shook his head. "Never met him. Can't say I'm sorry about that after what happened."

I could understand that. "Tell me more about the bench."

He cleared his throat, spat off into the distance, and spoke again. "The summer Greg made this bench, Edna didn't seem to have the energy to fish and swim. They'd come down to the pond every day, but after a short time she'd say she was tired, and they'd go back to the cabin. I could see Greg was frustrated and considered offering to keep an eye on him so he could stay at the pond while she napped. But Greg was a clever boy and came up with a different solution. He told me he wanted to buy his mama a bench to sit on while he swam and fished. He didn't have the money for it, but I had scrap wood, so I offered to help him build one." He put his hand on the back of the bench and gave it a jiggle. "It's sturdy too. Sure, it's weathered a bit after thirty-some winters and summers, but she's still solid as the day we built her."

I sat down on the bench and ran my hand over the carving. Suddenly, I wanted to cry. "That's so sweet." I looked up at him. "It was thoughtful of Greg to want to make a bench for his mother, even if he did have an ulterior motive for doing so, and generous of you to help him."

He lifted a shoulder. "I didn't mind helping. It did my heart good to see how that boy took care of his mama. I knew Edna's husband was a truck driver and away from home a lot. It was evident Greg had taken on the responsibility of making sure his mother was well cared for when his dad was away at a very young age. It wasn't until later that I heard about Edna's husband killing those girls. As I said, I never met the man, but a sweeter woman and a more adorable child you'd be hard-pressed to find."

"Did you ever hear Greg or Edna refer to this spot as their special place?" Tony asked.

"Sure. Every time they came out here after that first time. They'd come into the diner almost every day for their boxed lunch. While they waited for it, they'd tell anyone who'd listen that they were going to spend the day in their special place. The two had a real bond. From what they told me, they spent time together hiking and fishing even when they weren't staying here during the summer months. They loved the outdoors and spending time together."

"Did either of them ever mention someone named Georgie to you?"

He shook his head. "Not that I recall."

"The name came up during our search for Greg," I explained. "It seems he taught Greg to shoot."

"Boy never mentioned he liked to shoot back then. At least not to me. Might have come later."

"I suppose." I glanced at Tony. "If nothing else, we can show up here at noon on Sunday. If this is the place Chip plans to meet his mother, at least we can explain why she couldn't be here."

Tony nodded.

"I'll keep an eye out for the boy, although I guess he's not a boy any longer," he offered. "If you want to leave a number, I can call you if he shows up." He lowered his head. "It really is a damn shame. Seems like the father didn't just kill those women. He killed the bond between Greg and Edna as well."

We headed back down the trail, and Tony and I decided to have a meal at the little diner before we drove back to White Eagle. As it turned out, the End of the Trail Diner was pet friendly, so we ordered some food, then led the dogs to the vacant outdoor patio to eat our meal.

I sat back and looked up at the sky, which had faded from blue to gray. I was sure it would be dark before we made it home, but for now, I enjoyed the last glimpse of daylight. I inhaled deeply, sniffing the smell of woodsmoke from some nearby campfires. The sound of crickets welcoming the evening, combined with the soft breeze that caressed my face, had me feeling liquid and relaxed.

Tony was lost in his own thoughts, sitting silently beside me. I hadn't had the opportunity to camp much as a child, but tonight, with the wonderful smell of greasy burgers coming from the kitchen and the buzz of insects as they swarmed around the patio lights, I remembered that one perfectly spectacular fishing trip I'd taken with my father.

"Is everything okay?" I asked in a soft voice.

"I guess," he answered.

"Chip?"

He shook his head. "We're doing everything we can. I hope we find him, but if we don't, I'll know we tried." Tony laced the fingers of his left hand with my right.

"Being here, with the smell of campfires and the sound of crickets, I'm reminded of the fishing trip I took with my father. I remember we stopped at a place much like this on our way up to the lake where we stayed that week. Everything was just the same, right down to the creaky screen door, the sound of insects being fried by the porch light, and the smell of greasy burgers and home-sliced fries."

Tony squeezed my hand. "Isn't that a happy memory?"

I leaned my head on Tony's shoulder. "My memories of that week are happy. It's just that I'm finding it hard to reconcile the memory of a man who was so much fun with someone who was capable of faking his death and leaving his family to fend for themselves while he started another life."

Tony turned and kissed me on the forehead. "I'm sorry."

"Yeah. I know." I felt tears pushing against the back of my eyes. I took a deep breath and let it out slowly.

"We can stop looking," Tony said.

"No. I need to know." I sat up and turned so I could look at Tony. "It's just that being here, in this moment, and realizing Mike has a lot more happy memories of Dad than I do, makes me wonder how he's going to take it if he ever finds out what we know."

Tony didn't say anything. He squeezed my hand one more time, then let it go when the creaky screen door announced the waitress, bringing the greasy burgers and fries we'd been waiting for.

Chapter 14

Thursday, May 10

Mike had done some research and found birth records for both Edna and Chester Townsend in Cottonwood Falls, Kansas. Edna's brother, as it turned out, had left Cottonwood Falls after graduating high school. He'd drifted from place to place, working as a laborer. He'd never married or had children, and according to the folks Mike spoke to, he died young. Mike poked around a bit more, but it seemed no one knew what had happened to Edna after she married the stringent man who, it was rumored, bore the sign of the devil.

We'd been looking for Chip for a week but all we really had was the bench he'd made for his mother. I hoped we were correct, and the bench was the place he'd referred to in his letter; otherwise, I had no idea how we'd find Chip to inform him of his mother's passing. It occurred to me to try to track down the rest of the teens in the photo with Chip, and I'd worked on that the previous day. I'd spoken to Sue Wade, Mike to Rupert Hanson. Four of the others had long since moved on from White Eagle, which left only Tippy Tipton. He worked at the bowling alley and said he'd known Chip in high school but hadn't seen or heard from him since he'd left town a quarter century before.

It really did seem as if Chip Townsend had disappeared.

With Mother's Day only a few days away, the volume of mail had increased to the point where today was a two-mailbag day, and the coming ones would probably be the same. As I did every time I had a double bagger, I started my route in the middle, doing the north half of town in the morning and the south after lunch.

"Morning," I greeted Aunt Ruthie when I entered the diner with the day's mail. "Is Mom around?"

"She called Wanda to come in to cover for her. She's taking the day off."

I frowned. "Day off? Is she sick?"

Ruthie grinned a little knowing half smile that immediately informed me something was up. "No. She's not sick."

"Then why did she take the day off?" I asked, as a lead ball settled into the pit of my stomach.

"She has a gentleman friend visiting. She decided she wanted to have extra time to spend with him because he's in town so rarely."

My hand flew to my throat. "Romero? Is Romero here?"

Ruthie nodded with a little wink. "Seems he had some business in the area."

I wanted to panic but didn't, which, as it turned out, was a good thing. I needed time to think before I said anything to Aunt Ruthie— or anyone, for that matter—and she was already looking at me oddly.

She patted my arm. "Tess honey, I know it must be odd for you to have your mother dating someone, but your father's been gone a lot of years, and a woman has needs."

I squeezed my eyes shut. I didn't want to think about my mother's needs.

"Will she be in tomorrow?" I asked.

"I suspect she will." Ruthie put an arm around me. "I believe Mr. Montenegro is just in town for the day."

I placed a hand on my pale cheek. A day was enough if a man had homicide on his mind.

"I guess I might not have handled that the way I should," Aunt Ruthie said. "I can see I upset you, and that wasn't my intention. Would you like to talk about it?"

"No." I set the mail I'd brought in on the counter. "I'm fine, and I have a route to do. I'd best get to it." I turned and walked to the door with Tilly on my heels. Once I made it safely down the street, I pulled out my cell and called Tony. "Romero Montenegro is in town."

Tony didn't answer right away.

"What are we going to do?" I demanded. "He's with my mother at this very moment."

"Take a deep breath," Tony advised. "Romero being in town when we don't know whether he's guilty of killing his fiancée is unexpected and not ideal, but even if he was guilty, that doesn't mean your mother is in any danger."

"How can you say that?" I screeched in a voice so high, I didn't recognize it as my own.

"If he killed his fiancée—and I'm not saying he did—there must have been extenuating circumstances. It's not like he's left a trail of bodies in his wake over the past seven years. I doubt he's come all the way from Italy to do harm to a woman with whom he's only been engaged in a casual relationship."

I took a deep breath, as Tony suggested. "You may have a point. It doesn't make sense that he'd hurt my mother. He barely knows her. Still, I don't like this one bit. We have to do something."

"When can you take a lunch break?" Tony asked.

I glanced at my watch. "I usually take it in about two hours, but I can really take it whenever I like."

"Two hours is good. Meet me at the little park in the center of town then. I'll call my friend with the connections to see if I can hurry him up a bit, given the situation. And I'll check out a few other things that have occurred to me."

I had no idea how I was going to go about my route when my mother might literally be sleeping with a killer, but Tony had a point about Romero not having motive or intent where my mother was concerned. "Okay. Two hours. Don't be late."

I hung up and put my phone in my pocket. Then I bent over and buried my face in Tilly's neck. I tried to get my imagination under control, but all I could see when I closed my eyes was Romero's long, lean fingers wrapped around my mother's neck. I took my phone back out and called my mother. She didn't pick up her home phone, so I tried her cell.

"Tess. Is everything okay?" Mom asked.

"I'm fine but worried. Aunt Ruthie told me you didn't go into work today." I decided not to tell her that she'd let it slip she was with Romero. I wondered if she'd lie.

"No need to worry. I'm fine. Remember my friend from Italy?"

"Romero?"

"Yes, Romero. He's in the States on business. I wanted to spend some time with him, so I asked Wanda to cover for me."

"I called your house, but there was no answer."

"That's because I'm not at home. Romero and I are in Kalispell."

"Are you sure you should have just leave town with a man you barely know?"

Mom chuckled. "Romero is in town for the day, so we decided to go out for lunch and a drive."

"Lunch and a drive?"

"We're going to have lunch at that café I like so much, then maybe take a drive around the lake. It's such a beautiful day, it'd be a shame to waste it."

A drive around the lake sounded safe enough. I forced the panic from my voice. "That sounds fun. Will you be at work tomorrow?"

"I plan to be. Romero has business in Spokane tomorrow, so he'll be leaving early in the morning. The only reason I took today off was because we had such a short time to visit."

I let out a long breath. "Okay. I'm sorry I was worried and interrupted your date. Have a wonderful day." I hung up, then hugged my phone to my chest.

If Mom and Romero really were in Kalispell, I probably didn't need to worry about her today. Now all I had to do, I decided, was come up with an excuse to stop by my mother's that evening.

My mind was elsewhere, but I'd been doing this route for so long, I could do it in my sleep. I plastered on a fake smile and prepared a canned response to allow myself to hurry along should anyone attempt to make small talk. I wanted to get as much done as quickly as I could before lunch so I'd have as much time as I needed to work on the mystery of Luciana Parisi's death.

Tony was waiting in the park when Tilly and I arrived. In addition to his laptop, he had a bag from the deli down the street and two colas. My heart filled with gratitude at the ease with which he dropped whatever it was he'd planned to do that day to come running the minute I needed him. I owed him so much more than mere thanks, but right then, that was all I had to give him.

"Thanks for meeting me," I said before kissing him on the cheek and taking a seat at a picnic table.

"You know I'll come running whenever you need me." Tony handed me a paper-wrapped sandwich. "Eat this while we talk. This is, after all, your lunch break."

I looked at the wrapped package in my hand. My stomach rumbled. I wanted to say I wasn't hungry, but Tony would know better. Besides, he'd gone to all the trouble to buy the dang thing, the least I could do was try to choke down a few bites. I unwrapped the sandwich and took a small bite. Turkey, no mayo, extra pickles; just the way I liked it. "Do you have news?" I asked after swallowing and taking a sip of my cola.

"Yes and no." Tony opened his laptop. He had some sort of satellite internet that allowed him to get online anywhere. He logged on while I took another bite of the sandwich. "I spoke to my friend with the connections, asking if he'd had a chance to look in to things for me. He said he'd managed to speak to one of the men who investigated the murder seven years ago. Before Longorian confessed, it was this man's opinion it was Luciana's brother, Stefano, who'd killed her, although he was never able to prove it."

I frowned. "Her brother? Why?"

"It turns out, the same year Romero and Luciana became engaged, the Montenegro Winery took first place in the regional wine competition over the Parisi Winery, which had won the competition the previous five years. There was wide speculation among the management of the Parisi Winery that Luciana had shared with her fiancé the Parisi family recipe that had helped them win the competition in the past. Stefano insisted Romero's family had used the recipe he'd stolen to make adjustments to his wine to take back the title the two families had been fighting over for a century."

"But to kill your own sister over a wine competition?"

"I know it seems hard to believe, but there wasn't just a business rivalry between the two families but a century of hatred as well. A hatred that runs so deeply isn't easily dispelled. According to the investigator, Luciana's father and brother all but disowned her when she became engaged to a Montenegro."

I took a moment to consider this. It made me feel so sick, I had to push my sandwich aside. "Okay, so Luciana was murdered and her father blamed Romero, who claimed to be innocent but couldn't provide a solid alibi. The investigator didn't really suspect Romero because he thought Luciana's brother did it and didn't push the matter. Why did the investigator consider Stefano a suspect in the first place? He must have had more to base his suspicion on than anger between brother and sister."

"It seems Stefano had a record. A history of meeting frustration with violence. He'd been arrested seven times for beating someone to the point of unconsciousness. In all seven cases, financial compensation was offered to the victim and Stefano avoided jailtime. Those close to Stefano were loyal to him, probably partially out of fear. The investigator was trying to find proof that Stefano was guilty of the murder when Longorian confessed, and the investigation into Stefano was dropped. When Longorian died and the case was reopened, the investigator picked up where he'd left off and began speaking to people connected with Stefano. Most wouldn't talk, but the investigator found one vineyard worker—a man who'd worked for the Parisis for over forty years—who was willing to make an anonymous statement. He said Luciana came to the vineyard on the night she died. She met her father in the caverns, where they aged the wine. He didn't hear what was said, but he sensed something was wrong and stayed to watch. An hour later, Luciana came out of the cavern, got into her car, and drove away. Stefano, who had been lurking nearby, got into his own car and followed her. The vineyard worker had no idea what happened afterward, but he'd passed Stefano as he walked to the parking area, and he said he was obviously enraged. So enraged that he was pretty sure Stefano hadn't even seen him."

"I guess that would make Stefano a suspect. Were there others?"

"My contact said the local police looked at five people. In the end, they had it narrowed down to Stefano and Romero, but they never found proof that either was guilty. Then Longorian confessed, and they stopped looking."

I let everything Tony had said sink in. If Luciana had given away family secrets, and by doing so hurt the business, I could see why her father and brother might be angry with her, but kill her?

"I know Luciana died in her home. Was there sign of forced entry?" I asked.

Tony typed some commands into his computer, then pulled up a file. "I managed to obtain the original homicide report. According to the investigator, the front door was unlocked and the security system turned off when her body was found. The report doesn't say whether they believed she hadn't turned on the security system and locked the door when she came home, or if someone unlocked the door, turned off the system, killed her, and then left without locking up behind them."

"It sounds like they're no closer to solving the case now than they were seven years ago." I bent my arms so my elbows were on the table and groaned.

"Again, yes and no. My contact says there's buzz that there might be new evidence. But it's all very hush-hush. He said he'd poke around and let me know if he comes up with anything."

I put my hand on Tony's. "Thanks for digging into this. I'm not loving the fact that Romero is in town, but my mom said he's leaving early in the morning. Hopefully, this short visit won't be repeated until after Luciana's murder is solved."

Tony squeezed my hand. "Finish your sandwich. I know when you get stressed you forget to eat, but you need to keep up your energy."

"Yes, Mom." I smiled and took a bite of my sandwich.

Tony unwrapped his sandwich and began to eat as well. "I thought I might head over to finish your patio garden as long as I'm in town."

"Fine by me. The spare key is under the rock, where it always is."

"Don't you think you should move it from time to time?"

"Why? The only people who ever use it are you and Mike. There's nothing of value in the cabin, so there's no reason for anyone to want to break in. Besides, I have two ferocious attack cats on duty, just in case."

Tony laughed. "Yes, I guess you do have a certain level of feline protection. Still, it might be best to put the spare key in a more secure location. In fact, maybe we should install a keypad on your door like I have on mine."

I took a sip of my soda. "You have thousands and thousands of dollars' worth of computer and electronic equipment justifying your high-tech security system. The entire contents of my cabin wouldn't appraise for half of just one of your gadgets. I think a key under a rock is fine."

"I was thinking more about the need to protect the people and animals who live in the cabin. Your place is pretty isolated."

"I'm fine. We're fine. We don't need some fancy security system."

Tony shrugged. "Okay. Whatever you think is best."

Chapter 15

Saturday, May 12

Saturday dawned bright and sunny, making it the perfect day for doggy speed dating. Brady had selected twelve dogs to participate, and the potential new parents had each been given the number of a pen from which to start their rotation. It was a fast-paced game, but it seemed humans and dogs alike were having a wonderful time. More than twelve humans showed up for the event, so Brady had needed to add a few additional stops— just rest stops, really—so the number of stops and the number of people matched up.

Each potential dog parent had filled out an application before the event, and it was my duty to review the applications, approve those I knew and felt comfortable with, and flag the applications of those I didn't know, so we could look in to their home environment and background. There were those who thought we went a bit overboard with our background checks, but Brady and I both felt it was our responsibility to make sure the dogs ended up in happy homes where they'd be well cared for.

"I've cleared thirteen of the fifteen applicants," I said to Brady as we waited for the people who showed up to complete the entire rotation. "There are two applicants I don't know, though they have local addresses: Silvia Waterman and Rafe Wharton. Do you know either of them?"

"I know Silvia. Her sheltie passed away a couple of months ago. She did everything possible to save her, and I could see they were well bonded. I think you can add her to the approved pile." Brady frowned. "The name Rafe Wharton doesn't ring a bell."

"It looks like he just moved to White Eagle a few weeks ago." I reviewed the entire application. "He lives in a cabin not far from mine." I looked at Brady. "Tony is at my place, working on some patio furniture. I'll call him to see if he can run by the cabin to check for the fence Mr. Wharton claims to have. If it checks out, maybe you can interview him if he decides to adopt today."

"Okay, that sounds good." Brady looked at his watch. "Did I tell you that Jimmy committed to adopting Jagger and Bowie?"

No." I smiled. "I'm so glad that worked out."

"I took your suggestion about having Jimmy come out and work with me and the boys this week. Once Jimmy and Destiny got in the water with the boys, it was obvious the chemistry between humans and dogs was strong. Jimmy and Destiny had the brothers on the SUP boards and sitting quietly by the end of the day. Jimmy is coming by this afternoon to complete the paperwork. If he shows up while I'm occupied, there's a folder with his name on it in the box under the table."

"Okay. If I see him, I'll get it to him."

Running an adoption clinic with fifteen humans looking at twelve dogs took a lot longer than either Brady or I had anticipated, so it was already late afternoon by the time the people who'd chosen dogs to adopt had been processed. Jimmy had shown up, filled out the paperwork, and headed to the shelter, where a volunteer waited to turn his new buddies over to him. I was sorry I hadn't had the chance to say good-bye to the brothers, but I figured they'd be hanging out at the beach with Jimmy and Destiny this summer, so I could stop by at some point to say hello to everyone.

"I think that was a success," Brady said as we loaded the three dogs that hadn't been adopted into Brady's van.

"It was really fun, and I'm happy with all the matches." I looked at the mixed breed dog I'd just loaded into the van. "I wonder if we should try selective training and adoption for Scooter. This is the third adoption event he's participated in and he still hasn't found a forever home."

"We need to quell his need to bark at everything, and he could probably benefit from some behavior training," Brady said. "I noticed a couple of people showed interest in him initially, before he decided to serenade us for thirty minutes straight."

"I'm game to work with him next week. I'd really love to find him a home. I'll bring Tilly. She's turning out to be a heck of a dog trainer."

Brady laughed. "Sounds good. How's Monday after you get off work?"

"That works." I closed the van door when all the dogs were inside. "I should get going. Have a good weekend."

"You too. And thanks again for everything."

I glanced in the rearview mirror as I pulled away. It had been an exhausting but wonderful day. There was something so rewarding about being instrumental in matching the right human with the right dog.

Tony was sitting on the deck steps sipping a beer when I arrived at the cabin. Tilly and Titan jogged over to greet me as I pulled into the drive and parked. A quick glance at the deck behind Tony revealed he'd painted not only the rocker but the hanging porch swing as well. I'd loved my little cabin from the moment I'd seen it, but now with my pretty blue deck furniture, which complemented the darker blue garden boxes filled with brightly colored flowers, it really felt like a home.

"Oh, Tony," I gushed. "It looks exactly the way I pictured it. It's perfect."

Tony smiled. "I thought things came out very well. You have an eye for color. When you first said you were going with blue I wasn't sure how I'd like it, but now that everything has been painted and the flowers are planted, I can see the picture you had in your mind was perfect. How was the adoption event?"

I sat down on the step next to Tony. I was itching to try out my newly painted chair, but I'd need to let it dry first. "It was really great. We managed to place nine of the twelve dogs with really good people."

"I'm glad to hear that. I hate to think of all the shelter animals out there waiting for forever homes."

"Yeah. It is sad. Brady has a new neuter-and-spay program he hopes will get more folks to become responsible pet owners. Not only is the procedure free for anyone who asks, but he's offering free shots and free checkups for a year to anyone who brings their pet in for alteration."

"Sounds like that might get him some attention."

"He just started the program at the beginning of the month, but he said he has more procedures scheduled than he and Lilly can manage. He's thinking of bringing in an intern to help out over the summer." I turned as my house phone rang. "I should get that. Then I'll grab my own beer and come back out to join you."

Inside, I picked up the handset to my landline.

"Hello, dear. How was the clinic?"

"It went really well," I said to my mother. "It was pretty exhausting, but nine dogs who didn't have homes this morning have them now."

"That's wonderful. Listen, I'm calling to let you know there'll be one more guest for dinner tomorrow. Romero finished his business in Spokane and has decided to come back to White Eagle for a few days before he goes home. He'll be here later this evening, so I invited him to join us tomorrow. I hope that's all right."

I wanted to say no, but how could I? "Of course that's fine. It is, after all, Mother's Day. Have you told Mike that Romero is in town?"

Mom hesitated and then said, "Not yet. You know how protective he is. I'm a little worried about how he'll react to my friendship with Romero. You've been so understanding, I hoped maybe you could pave the way, talk to him about the visit. He listens to you, and I'm not up for an argument about my social life."

I closed my eyes and counted to ten. I so didn't want to have this conversation with Mike. "Yeah, okay, I can do that if you'd like. You can consider it my Mother's Day gift to you because I never did get around to buying you anything."

Mom laughed. "Thank you, sweetheart. I knew I could count on you. Are we still on for one-thirty?"

I considered the fact that because we still hadn't tracked down Chip, Tony and I had decided to show up at the bench at noon and hope he was there. "Actually, I might need to move it back a bit. Tony and I are planning to try to meet Chip at noon. We aren't a hundred percent sure that's where he'll be expecting to meet his mother, but it's our best bet. Would it be okay if we had dinner a little later? Maybe three?"

"That would be fine with me. It's a nice thing you kids are doing. I'll see you tomorrow."

I hung up the phone. "Crap, crap, crap."

"Something wrong?" Tony, who was standing in the doorway, asked.

"That was my mom. Romero is coming back to White Eagle tonight. And if that weren't bad enough, my mom wants me to talk to Mike and smooth the way, so he won't make a scene tomorrow. I don't suppose you have any news on the Parisi investigation since we spoke?"

"Actually, I do. Let's take a walk and I'll bring you up to date."

"A walk sounds nice. Let me grab my other shoes."

Tony and I walked for a good five minutes, enjoying the perfection of the spring day, before either of us spoke. The warm weather had accelerated the snowmelt, and every river, stream, and seasonal creek was overflowing with the cool, clear water that ran down from the mountains. Titan and Tilly were having a wonderful time splashing in the shallow creeks and streams. We had decided to avoid the river, so we didn't need to worry about the dogs trying to cool off on a hot spring day.

"Okay, what do you know?" I asked after a few minutes longer.

"My contact said Luciana's brother was able to provide an alibi for the time of Luciana's murder. It seems after he left the vineyard behind Luciana, he went to visit his mistress, who, like he, was and still is married to someone else. During the initial investigation, he refused to provide an alibi. I guess this time he changed his mind."

"So now we're back to Romero as the only suspect?"

"No. In fact, an arrest has been made."

I stopped walking. "Really? Who?"

"The vineyard worker who told the police about Stefano in the first place. It occurred to the investigator that the timing of the eyewitness report was odd. Luciana was killed seven years ago. If this man, who'd been working for the Parisi family for decades, saw Stefano follow Luciana and believed he may have killed her, why did he wait so long to tell what he saw?"

"That's a good point," I said.

"The investigator looked into things a bit more closely and found the man was an oenologist."

"An oenologist? What's that?'

"Oenology, or enology, is the science of wine and winemaking. An oenologist is an expert. He wasn't simply an employee of the Parisi family; he was the person responsible for coming up with the specific recipe that had earned the Parisi Winery all those awards. Not only was it his formula Luciana had supposedly given to Romero, but as the oenologist for the winery, he received a percentage of the profit the winery made each year. After the Montenegro Vineyard won the regional competition, sales for Parisi wine declined."

"So he killed Luciana in a fit of rage," I concluded.

"Not exactly. After Luciana left the winery that night, he followed her. She went home, and he parked down the street, walked to the house, and knocked on the door. She opened it for him; why wouldn't she, when she'd known him all her life? They argued, and he pushed her. She hit her head and died. It appears as if Luciana's death was an accident. Still, instead of notifying the authorities, he left and went back to work. No one even knew he'd left the winery. He would have gotten away with it if he hadn't become nervous when the investigation was reopened and tried to frame Stefano. It was a dumb move on his part."

I frowned. "So why did Longorian take the fall for an employee of the Parisi Family Winery? It kind of made sense that he would confess to a manslaughter charge he wasn't responsible for if the primary suspect was not only a good friend but a man in a position to help him out financially but if it was a vineyard employee that was actually responsible for her death the whole thing makes no sense."

"Perhaps. But the individuals involved in the wine industry are a close knit community. It is possible that Luciano knew the man he covered for and was willing to take the rap for a payout. I guess at this point we'll never know."

"No I guess not. Still, I'm very relieved to know Romero wasn't the killer. Of course, that isn't going to make my discussion with Mike any easier. He's going to be blindsided by the whole thing,"

"He doesn't know about Romero at all?"

"No. I knew he'd freak out, so I didn't mention him, and Mom didn't either. But now that Romero's going to be in town tomorrow and she wants to bring him to dinner, it's time to fill Mike in."

Tony made a face.

"Exactly. Mike isn't going to be happy, and I was a fool to agree to be the one to tell him."

"Maybe he'll take it better than you think."

"And maybe pigs can fly." I pulled out my cell and took a deep breath. "I may as well get this over with."

Chapter 16

Sunday, May 13

Tony was carrying a gift when he arrived at my cabin the next day. Wrapped in blue paper and a giant red ribbon, it caught my attention immediately. "What is this?" I asked when he handed it to me. I stepped aside and let Tony through the door. "This is Mother's Day, and I'm not a mother."

Tony tossed his keys on the table near the front door, a habit I'd noticed he'd developed recently. "I know. Open it."

I ripped the paper from top to bottom and gasped. "Where did you get this?"

"I made it."

I looked at the large photo of the meadow with the old cabin, colorful flowers, and seasonal creek Tony and I had seen on our walk up to the waterfall. "You went back and took a photo?"

Tony nodded. "Is the frame okay?"

It was made of rustic wood and stained dark. It was exactly what I'd pictured in my head. "It's perfect. Absolutely perfect."

Tony held up a hammer and nail. "I can hang it for you."

I smiled and walked across the room. "Right here. I pictured it right here on this wall."

Tony pounded in the nail, hung the photo, and stood back.

"I love it." I turned and threw my arms around Tony's neck. "Really, really love it. Thank you so much." I leaned forward and impulsively kissed him on the lips. It was a quick kiss. Unplanned. Simple, and in many ways unspectacular. Yet it sent a volt of something I so didn't want to take the time to analyze through my body to my very core. I took a step back, trying desperately not to blush.

Tony looked as if he was going to say something but then didn't. He took his own step back and reminded me that we needed to get going if we were going to get up to the bench Chip had made for his mother by eleven-thirty. We'd decided to get there early so there wouldn't be any chance we'd miss him.

We'd decided to leave the dogs at the cabin. We weren't sure what to expect when we arrived at the little pond where a young Greg Fairchild had liked to fish and swim. We wouldn't be gone all that long, and Mike and Bree both planned to come to the cabin early to get a start on the preparations for the barbecue should we be detained.

"So, how's Mike today?" Tony asked as we drove out of town. As predicted, when I'd first told Mike about Romero the previous night, he'd gone ballistic.

"He seemed better when I spoke to him this morning. He'd not only had a chance to think about things, but he'd talked it over with Bree, and she made him look at things from a different perspective. Of course, he'd had no idea Romero's fiancée was murdered or that he'd been considered a suspect; I felt it best to keep that piece of information from him."

"I'm glad Bree was able to talk him down," Tony said. "It would have been a very uncomfortable afternoon today if he arrived on the warpath."

I turned slightly so I was facing him. "Do you think there's something between Mike and Bree?"

"What do you mean?"

"I'm not sure. They've known each other for most of their lives and mostly gotten along all right, but they've never spent time together with just the two of them. I suggested Mike ask her to dinner a week or so ago when I knew she was looking for something to do one night. They had a good time, which didn't surprise me. But what did surprise me is that ever since, they've been spending a lot of time together. I think there might be something going on there other than friendship."

Tony glanced at me out of the corner of his eye. "Would it matter if there were?"

I hesitated and looked out the windshield. "I don't know. Maybe. Bree's my best friend and Mike's my brother. I love them both and want them to be happy. But the idea of them being more than friends is really weird for me."

"Have you talked to either of them about it?"

I shook my head. "No. And I'm not going to. Not yet. For all I know, there's nothing going on and I'm freaking out for nothing. Sure, they've been spending a ridiculous amount of time together since that first dinner, but *we* spend a lot of time together and *we're* just friends. They could be just friends too." Tony didn't respond, so I went on. "I mean, it isn't like they've been doing anything really romantic. He fixed her fence and took her fishing. All very innocent, but I'm picking up a vibe." I turned once again and looked at Tony. "I'm good at picking up vibes of the romantic sort. Always have been. I really think there might be something there."

The oddest look washed over Tony's face.

"What?" I asked.

"I didn't say a thing."

"Maybe, but you had a look."

Tony lifted a shoulder. "I was just thinking that maybe you aren't as good about picking up vibes as you think you are."

I frowned. "Yeah. I guess you might be right. It'd be crazy if there were vibes between Mike and Bree after they'd been friends for so long."

"Yeah, crazy."

Tony pulled off the highway onto the road that led to the parking area provided for hikers. We got out and began to walk down the trail.

"I'm really nervous," I said when Tony laced his fingers with mine. "I'm not really sure why. I'm not even sure if I'm hoping Chip shows or not. Is that weird?"

Tony squeezed my hand slightly. "Not really. What started as a misdirected piece of mail has ended up being an emotional journey. And it's never fun to have to tell someone—even someone you don't know—that someone they love has died. Especially when we know Chip will never have the second chance he wrote about with his mother."

I felt emotion clog my throat. The meeting today, should there be one, really had all the makings of a very emotional moment. "Thank you."

"For what?" Tony asked.

"For helping me with this, no matter how it turns out. For putting your life on hold to be there for me this week." My voice caught just a bit. "For being you."

Tony stopped walking. He turned me so we were facing each other. I swear, it looked as if he had something heavy on his mind. He looked deeply into my eyes for several seconds, and then he glanced over my shoulder. He turned me so I was looking in the same direction he was.

"That must be him," I said when I saw a man with dark hair sitting on the bench.

"Are you ready for this?"

I nodded, taking a deep breath as I did. "As much as I'll ever be." My heart began to pound as I looked at the man. "I wonder how he's going to take it."

Tony put his arm around my shoulder and took a step forward. "I guess there's only one way to find out."

******

Later that afternoon, I sat with Bree in my newly painted swing. Romero and Mike had hit it off, and they were sitting with Mom, talking about the huge wine festival the Montenegro Winery held in the fall. Tony had taken Titan and Tilly for a walk, so we were spending a few minutes catching up.

"I'm glad Chip was okay after the initial shock," Bree said as we gently swayed forward and back.

"I could see he was upset, but there was something else in his eyes. Acceptance. The cabin he and his mom used to rent was vacant, so he made plans to stay there for a while. He's going to clean out the storage shed and see to any other loose ends Edna might have left behind. Hopefully, by the time he's ready to go home, he'll have made peace with the situation."

"Did you find out why he seemed to have disappeared for all those years?"

"He said he couldn't deal with the fallout from his father's legacy, so he took off. He drifted for a few years and then got a job on a private island in the Caribbean, working as a groundskeeper. He was there until a few months ago, when he decided it was time to grow up and come home. I feel really bad for him. He was dealt a tough lot in life, which he handled the best he could. He appeared to realize he caused his mother a lot of pain by leaving, and he feels guilty about that. I imagine it might take him some time to work through that."

The chain holding the swing to the overhead support creaked slightly as we rocked. The sound had a quaint, comfortable feel to it. It was calm and peaceful overlooking the meadow, with the mountains in the distance. As the minutes melded into one another, they created a contentment that wrapped its arms around me like a bear hug.

"I think I might have feelings for Mike." Bree breathed so softly that I wasn't certain if she had said the words or I'd imagined them.

"Feelings?"

Bree lowered her eyes. "I know it's crazy, and the feelings I think I'm having could be the result of a deep longing to have someone in my life." Bree looked up at me. "But this week, whenever he's been around, I've felt a rumbling in my stomach."

"Are you sure it isn't just indigestion?" I teased.

Bree laughed. "It's not indigestion. And I know that just because I have butterflies doesn't mean he sees me as anything more than his little sister's pesky friend. We've had a wonderful time this past week, but it's not like we have a relationship. We've never even kissed. I'm crazy to think he even knows I'm alive. Right?"

I thought back to Valentine's Day. The gifts he'd delivered to her anonymously to cheer her up for not having anyone in her life on the most romantic day of the year. I thought about the moodiness Frank had attributed to girl problems, an affliction my brother had never had before. I could discourage Bree, tell her that what she was feeling was probably nothing more than a reaction to the mess her love life had become since Donny. She'd believe me and most likely move on. And if she did, I wouldn't have to worry about my brother and my best friend getting into a messy entanglement. "You should tell him how you feel," I said instead. "I think he might be feeling those same butterflies. In fact, I think he might have been feeling them for quite some time."

"Really?" I felt a rush of emotion as Bree's face filled with hope. "You think so?"

I couldn't tell her about the gifts Mike had sent. It wasn't my secret to share. "Yeah." I reached out and grabbed Bree's hand. "I think so. Mike and I are close, and sometimes a sister just knows those things."

Bree looked to the others sitting around the table, chatting. I followed her gaze. Mom and Romero stood up, as if they were saying their good-byes to Mike. "Maybe I'll see if Mike wants to take a walk. I'm afraid if I don't tell him now, I'll chicken out and never do it."

"Go ahead. Mom and Romero are leaving, and Tony should be back soon. He can help me with the cleanup."

Bree hugged me. "Thank you."

I hugged Bree back. "For what?"

"For always being there for me. For putting my needs in front of your own. For understanding how I feel and what it is I want to say even when the right words elude me."

I touched Bree's arm with my hand. "Of course I'm always there for you. You're my best friend. Now go talk to Mike before you talk yourself out of it."

I watched Bree as she walked across the grass. She paused briefly to say good-bye to my mother and Romero, then continued to where Mike was standing. She said something to him. He nodded and took her hand. They never looked back as they walked together into the forest. As I watched them stroll away, I wondered how things would turn out. Would I look back on this moment and wish I'd tried to convince Bree that her feelings were a schoolgirl crush? Or would I realize this moment was *the* moment when two people I loved very much found each other?

Tony returned with the dogs shortly after everyone left. He sat down in the swing next to me. I laid my head on his shoulder as the gentle breeze of the spring day caressed my cheeks. Tony entwined the fingers of his left hand with my right hand as we rocked back and forth.

"Where did everyone go?"

"Mom and Romero left, and Mike and Bree went for a walk," I said.

"It's a beautiful day for a walk."

"It is. But I think the walk had more to do with talking than walking." I took a slow breath and let it out. "Bree told me that she has feelings for Mike, and I'm pretty sure he has feelings for her too."

Tony's hand tightened slightly on mine. "And how do you feel about that?"

I frowned. "I'm not sure. I love Bree and I love Mike, but I'm scared." I was quiet for a beat. "Do you think people who are friends, who have been friends for a very long time, can ever be anything more?"

Tony stopped rocking. He took my chin in his hand and looked deeply into my eyes. "I absolutely think friendship can be the basis for the most powerful love two people can have."

I felt a tingling in my own stomach. I knew I should say something, but I had no idea what that something would be. I wasn't sure if Tony was talking about Bree and Mike or something else entirely, but I was both too moved and too scared to ask.

Next from Kathi Daley Books

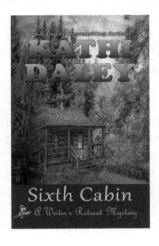

Preview

Monday, January 29

Most every Monday evening, the group of writers who live and write at the Gull Island Writers' Retreat meet in the main house, where I, Jillian Hanford, live with my brother, resort owner Garrett Hanford and paranormal writer Clara Kline. The other writers, who live in cabins scattered around the oceanfront property, gather, not only to socialize, but to discuss whichever mystery the Mastermind Group is currently investigating. This week, one of our newer residents, Nicole Carrington, had asked to present a mystery to us. Nicole had moved to the resort two months before in the hope of picking up the trail of her half sister, Emily Halliwell, who ran away from home when she was just sixteen but agreed to maintain contact with her sister via a weekly photo. The last photo Nicole had received arrived on May 8.

"Okay everyone, let's get right to it," I said once the meal I'd served had been eaten and we'd gathered in a large circle near the stone fireplace to discuss this week's case. "As I've already mentioned, Nicole has a mystery she'd like to present to the group. I thought it best if we gave her the floor so she can lay the groundwork. Please feel free to ask any questions you have."

In the two months Nicole had been living at the resort, she'd made it clear us that she wasn't interested in socializing or engaging in any shared investigations. The fact that she was here tonight had a lot of us feeling uncertain, some of us suspicious.

"Thank you for agreeing to hear my case." Nicole, a tall woman with a thin frame dressed in black dress slacks and a white button-down blouse smiled weakly. Her pale complexion set off her black hair and huge brown eyes, which had taken on a serious expression when she took the floor. "As I've already explained to Jill, the reason I came to the island wasn't, as I told everyone, to do research for a novel, but to research a missing person. Her name is Emily. She's my half sister and I haven't heard from her since May."

No one spoke, but I could see Nicole had everyone's attention. The group was made up of wonderful people, but Nicole had gone to such lengths to push everyone away that I wasn't sure how she would be received. Still, I hoped they would find it in their hearts to forgive Nicole and rise to the challenge of locating a teen who could very well need our help.

Nicole made eye contact with each person in the room as she continued. "Emily and I aren't close. She's the product of my mother's second marriage, to a man I've only met once. My mother is a troubled woman. I've only spoken to her a handful of times since I was put into foster care when I was twelve." She paused and took a breath. I couldn't imagine how hard this must be for her. "When Emily was born I was fifteen and living with my third foster family. I was taken from my mother when it became apparent she didn't have what it took to care for or supervise me. I was told that once she completed a series of tasks determined by the court, I'd be returned to her." Nicole cleared her throat, then took a sip of water from the glass on the table near her. "In the beginning, I believed she would fight for me, so I hoped and waited. But as the days turned to weeks, and the weeks turned to months, I began to fear she had moved on without me. When Emily was born, it finally sank in that the person I'd depended on more than anyone in the world was too busy marrying another man and having another baby to even remember the child she'd left behind."

I put a hand to my heart. It was obvious Nicole was still angry about the situation. Not that I blamed her. She appeared to be a very private person and I was willing to bet it had taken her a lot of courage to admit to her feelings of betrayal and, I was sure, inadequacy.

Nicole continued. "After I reached my eighteenth birthday and was free to make my own choices, I got a job, worked hard, and cut my mother out of my life completely. I figured if she didn't have time for me, I didn't have time for her. I didn't see or hear from her or my sister for almost nine years. I saw Emily for the first time at my grandmother's when she was twelve. After I spoke to her, I realized I'd had the better childhood. I won't say we became great friends, but we did begin to text each other from time to time, and I made a point of sending her a gift on her birthday and for Christmas."

Nicole cleared her throat and looked nervously around the room before she continued. "Emily called me on the night she left home. She told me that her father had been beating her and she was done. I didn't blame her for wanting out and offered to let her stay with me. I even offered to drive to Bangor, where she lived with our mother and her father, and pick her up. She said she was grateful for the offer, but she'd met a boy and was in love. She wanted to start a life with this guy, who I know only as Slayer."

I cringed. The name Slayer didn't suggest a guy who would act responsibly and take care of Emily.

Nicole resumed her story. "Emily knew I was worried about her being on her own, so she agreed to send me a selfie once a week to prove she was safe and happy. And she did. Every Monday, up until May 15."

"There was no photo on May 15?" Jackson Jones, a nationally acclaimed author, local newspaper owner, and my boyfriend, asked.

"There was no photo on May 15 or ever again," Nicole confirmed. "The last photo I received was sent on May 8. It took me months to figure out where the last photo was taken, but after more than four months of searching for Emily, following every lead I could carve out of the few clues I had, I determined it was taken right here on Gull Island. Right here at this resort."

"And you had no idea at all where she might have gone after she left here?" Clara, a self-proclaimed psychic and the author of paranormal mysteries, asked.

Nicole shook her head. "None. When she missed sending me a photo for the second week in a row, I grew worried."

"Did you call the police?" Alex Cole, a fun and flirty millennial and nationally best-selling author, asked.

Nicole nodded. "When I hadn't heard from her for three weeks, I called the police in Maine and tried to report her as a missing person. Of course, the first question I was asked was when I had last seen Emily. I had to say it had been over a year since I'd seen her, and I tried to explain about the photos. Finally, I managed to get someone to at least go to speak to Emily's parents. Our mother assured the police that Emily wasn't missing; she'd run away. She painted a picture of a troubled girl who was in to drugs and other illegal activity who had abandoned her loving and dedicated parents despite their effort to get help for her. The officer who spoke to my mother and her pond scum of a husband did file a report, but Emily was listed as a runaway, not as a missing person. I'm pretty sure no one took the time to look for her."

Alex leaned forward, resting his forearms on his thighs and letting his hands hang between them. "You said you hadn't seen Emily in over a year and you weren't really close to her. You also said at the beginning that Emily had run away, so the way police classified her disappearance from her family home was accurate. Are you certain Emily didn't just get tired of sending you photos as she made a life with this new guy of hers?"

"No," Nicole admitted. "I'm not certain Emily is in trouble. She may very well have just grown tired of placating me and stopped bothering with the photos. I've tried texting the phone she sent me the photos from hundreds of times, but they remain undelivered. It's possible she lost or damaged the phone, which might also explain why the photos stopped so abruptly. But I need to know that she's okay." Nicole looked Alex in the eye. "If she were your sister, what would you do?"

Alex sat back in his chair, using one hand to swipe his longish hair back from over his eyes. "I guess, like you, I'd need to know for certain. Which leads to my next question. You've been here for months; why didn't you ask for our help before now?"

"Honestly," Nicole looked around the room, "I didn't trust you. Any of you. The last place my sister was seen was here, and then she disappeared. After I got to know everyone, I could see none of you were responsible for her disappearance. I've exhausted every lead, which were slim to begin with. I need your help."

Alex smiled a crooked little smile. "Okay. That's good enough for me."

"You said you've exhausted every clue," George Baxter, a seasoned author of traditional whodunits, began. "Exactly what clues have you found to this point?"

"Not a lot, I'm afraid, but I have a general feel for the route Emily took. I went back through the photos and tried to figure out where they were all taken. It wasn't easy because they all had nondescript scenery in the background, but I caught a break and found one of the places she stayed. She had moved on by the time I arrived, of course, but I was able to trace the route she and her boyfriend took to the location of the next photo. Based on things she said to people I spoke to, I could move from the location of one photo to the next. I continued to follow them until I arrived on Gull Island."

"Do you have a copy of the last photo Emily sent?" Jack asked.

Nicole held up a photo she'd had enlarged for the meeting. It featured a smiling young girl with long dark hair and shining blue eyes. She was standing in front of a wooden door with the number six on it.

"*Save the girl, save the girl*," said Blackbeard, Garrett's talkative parrot.

Garrett chuckled. "Yep that does seem to be the point of this discussion, and yes, the cabin in the photo is one of ours before we remodeled."

Nicole looked directly at Garrett, who was sitting in his wheelchair next to Clara. "The reason I wanted to rent a cabin here in the first place was because my sister's trail died here. When I first contacted Jill, I hoped you would recognize Emily, but then I learned you'd already suffered a stroke and were in the hospital this past May."

"Yes. I'm sorry," Garrett said with sympathy. "The resort was closed and boarded up after my stroke in late April, until a friend arrived to open it up in June."

"I've since learned that, which is why I'm here this evening. I need your help." Nicole looked around the room. "All of your help. I don't know where Emily is. I don't know if she's dead or alive. What I do know is that this resort is the last place she took a selfie. It's the last place I know she was."

The room fell into silence as everyone processed Nicole's words.

"This is going to be a difficult case," Jack said. "We'll need to ask tough questions. I suspect your instinct might be to protect your sister from information you think she might not want shared, but even small details could be important."

Nicole nodded. "I understand. I'm prepared to be transparent. I just want to find Emily and take her home." Nicole swiped angrily at a tear that slipped down her cheek.

I stood up to divert the group's attention to give Nicole a chance compose herself. From what I knew about her, she wasn't comfortable with public displays of emotion. "Let's come up with a plan. A place to start. We all have our specialties; let's come up with a plan to use them."

Brit Baxter, a novice blond-haired writer of chick lit and George's niece, began. "I can check the usual social media sites to see if photos or mentions of

Emily pop up. I can run a Google search for general information, and if you have a list of the places she visited prior to her arrival here, I can research them as well,"

"And I'll consult my cards," Clara offered. She looked at Nicole. "Do you have something personal of hers? Perhaps a hairbrush?"

Nicole looked like she might refuse but then changed her mind and agreed to get something to Clara right away. It seemed obvious to me that Nicole would depend on logic over feelings and clairvoyance, but she also was determined to do whatever was asked of her.

"Alex and I can work together to dig into the backgrounds of both Emily and this Slayer," George volunteered. He glanced at Alex, who nodded.

"I'll pull up as much as I can from news articles that may tie in and be relevant," Jack spoke up. "And Jill and I will also sit down with Nicole and work up a detailed timeline. Once we have that, it may be necessary for someone to go back and reinterview anyone individuals Nicole has already spoken to."

"I have time and am happy to travel if need be," I offered.

"I'll show Emily's photo to others on the island," Garrett volunteered. "I know a lot of people. Someone must have seen her."

"I'll take you," Clara offered. "I can drive."

I couldn't help but notice the way Garrett smiled at Clara. It almost seemed as if something was going on between them, but I had no proof of anything more than friendship and it wasn't my business.

I was about to ask Nicole if she had anything she wanted to add at this point when my best friend, romance writer Victoria Vance walked into the house with our temporary resident, Abby Boston, and her nieces and nephews.

"Sorry to interrupt," Vikki said. "Abby has been released from the hospital and I want to get her settled." Vikki had jumped right in with the kids when it became apparent the very pregnant Abby was going to need help. Lord knew she'd had a tough time of it. First, Abby's sister had died, leaving her with her four children to raise, and then Abby's husband had been murdered. To top it all off, shortly before her husband's death, Abby had found out she had a child of her own on the way. When Abby ended up in the hospital with complications, we'd decided that Abby and the kids should stay with us until after the baby was born.

"I'm glad you're home." I smiled at Abby.

She smiled shyly in return.

"I'll help you get everyone settled," Brit popped up. She turned to Nicole. "Don't worry. We'll find your sister."

Nicole sent Brit a look of thanks, then turned back to the rest of the group. "Thank you all for agreeing to do what you can. It means more to me than I can say. I've never had anyone I could depend on. You all are so very lucky to have one another."

******

After everyone returned to their own cabins or rooms, Jack and I took our golden retriever Kizmet—Kizzy for short—out for a walk. Kizzy had stayed with me while Jack's mother had been visiting him, but now that she'd gone, Kizzy was back to living with him. I found I was really going to miss her. I'd never wanted a dog before, but now that I'd spent time with one, I realized how the furry little creatures could burrow into your heart, filling in all the dark and empty spaces.

"I spoke to Nicole before she left," I said as we walked hand in hand along the beach. "She agreed to meet with us in the morning. As we'd already discussed, I told her nine o'clock would work best for us. She'll be ready with copies of maps, photos, and notes to share."

"This isn't going to be easy," Jack cautioned as the waves from the calm sea lapped up onto the shore.

"I know. I think she realizes that too. But God, Jack. A sixteen-year-old girl out on her own with some random guy who might not be trustworthy. We have to try."

Jack squeezed my hand. "And we will. If she can be found, we'll find her."

"You think she's dead," I said in a flat tone.

Jack stopped walking and looked at me. "I think she's either dead or for some reason doesn't want to be found. I can't think of any other reason she'd stop sending the photos all of a sudden the way she did."

Kizzy brought me a stick. I picked it up and tossed it. "She could have been in an accident. She could have amnesia."

Jack put his arm around my shoulders and began walking again. "Yes, there is that. Or she could have been kidnapped. If she's being held captive, we may be able to find the clues we need to track her down."

I laid my head on Jack's shoulder. "I know the odds are that if we solve the mystery, we'll do it by finding something tragic. I hope with my whole heart that isn't true, but it seems to me if someone close to me was missing, I'd want to know. One way or the other, I'd want to know."

Jack kissed the side of my face. "Yeah. Me too."

We continued to walk in silence, each lost in our own thoughts. After a while, Jack spoke. "You said tonight that if it was determined that reinterviewing people Nicole had already spoken to as she traveled south was necessary, you'd do it."

I nodded. "Garrett is doing better, and Clara helps him out with whatever he needs anyway. Brit and Vikki seem to have taken over as caregivers for Abby and the kids, and I know Alex has a deadline he's been struggling with. I suppose George might have time to take a road trip, but I'd worry about him going on his own. He's not exactly a spring chicken. I'm between projects right now, I have interview skills from my days as a reporter, and I want to help. I think it should be me."

"I agree. What I was going to say is that if you go, I'm going with you."

"But you have the paper."

"I can do what I need to do from the road once I get the paper out on Wednesday with the help of my part-timers. I know you're a capable adult and I'm not trying to smother you, but I'd feel more comfortable if I went with you."

I looked at the feisty puppy that was sitting at our feet, waiting for one of us to bend down and pick up the stick. "What about Kizzy?"

"We'll bring her."

I bent down, picked up the stick, and tossed it. "Okay. If, after speaking to Nicole, we feel there would be benefit in reinterviewing the people she's already spoken to, we'll all go. You, me, and the dog."

Recipes

Italian Chicken—submitted by Sharon Guagliardo
Chicken Tetrazzini—submitted by Pam Curran
Chili Spaghetti—submitted by Patty Liu
Peanut Butter Swirl Brownies—submitted by Darla Taylor

Italian Chicken

Submitted by Sharon Guagliardo

1 med. red pepper, chopped
1 med. onion, chopped
7–10 mushrooms, sliced
3 boneless chicken breast, sliced lengthwise, then cubed
Hunt's Stewed Tomatoes
Diced fresh parsley
Diced slivered garlic (3–4 cloves)
½ lemon
Pinch of sugar

Melt 1 tbs. butter-flavored Crisco in pan. Sauté peppers, onions, mushrooms, and chicken until onions are translucent. Add stewed tomatoes, parsley, garlic, lemon, and sugar.

Italian seasoning (7–9 shakes):
⅛ tsp. chili powder
Coarse black pepper

Simmer 10 minutes. Add sugar, stir in, and serve. Good on fettuccine, egg noodles, or rice.

Serves 4.

Chicken Tetrazzini

Submitted by Pam Curran

1 chopped onion
2 sliced celery sticks
2 tbs. bacon grease
½ lb. Velveeta cheese
1 can cream of mushroom soup
½ tsp. salt
¼ tsp. black pepper
3 cups chicken broth
1 boiled, boned chicken
10 oz. cooked spaghetti
Slivered almonds

Sauté onion and celery in bacon grease. Add cheese and soup and cook until cheese melts. Add salt and pepper. Then add broth and chicken, stirring mixture. Add cooked spaghetti. Turn into greased baking dish. Top with almonds and bake at 350 degrees for 45–50 minutes.

Chili Spaghetti Casserole

Submitted by Patty Liu

8 oz. spaghetti
1 lb. lean ground beef
1 med. onion, chopped
Salt to taste
Black pepper to taste
1 can chili with beans, undrained
1 can Italian-style stewed tomatoes, undrained
1½ cups shredded sharp cheddar cheese, divided
½ cup sour cream
1½ tsp. chili powder
¼ tsp. garlic powder

Preheat oven to 350 degrees. Spray a 2 x 9 x13-in. baking dish with Pam Original. Cook pasta according to package directions; drain and place in prepared baking dish. In a large skillet, brown meat and onion; drain. Add salt and pepper and stir in chili, tomatoes, 1 cup of cheese, sour cream, and chili and garlic powders. Add chili mixture to pasta and stir until pasta well coated; sprinkle with remaining cheese. Cover lightly with foil and bake 30 minutes or until hot and bubbly; let stand 5 minutes before cutting into squares.

Serves 6 to 8

Peanut Butter Swirl Brownies

Submitted by Darla Taylor

2 cups sugar
1 cup (2 sticks) butter or margarine, melted
2 tbs. water plus 1 tbs. added during mixing if needed
2 large eggs
3 tsp. vanilla extract
1½ cups flour
¾ cup cocoa
½ tsp. baking powder
¼ tsp. salt
6 tbs. (or to taste) peanut butter (I use crunchy)
Powdered sugar

Preheat oven to 350 degrees.

Grease 2 x 9 x 13 baking pan.

Combine sugar, butter, and water in large bowl. Stir in eggs and vanilla extract.

Combine flour, cocoa, baking powder, and salt in a medium bowl. Stir into sugar mixture. Spread into prepared pan.

Place peanut butter in six mounds across top of brownie batter. Using a butter knife, cut through the peanut butter and swirl throughout the batter.

Books by Kathi Daley

Come for the murder, stay for the romance.

Zoe Donovan Cozy Mystery:
Halloween Hijinks
The Trouble With Turkeys
Christmas Crazy
Cupid's Curse
Big Bunny Bump-off
Beach Blanket Barbie
Maui Madness
Derby Divas
Haunted Hamlet
Turkeys, Tuxes, and Tabbies
Christmas Cozy
Alaskan Alliance
Matrimony Meltdown
Soul Surrender
Heavenly Honeymoon
Hopscotch Homicide
Ghostly Graveyard
Santa Sleuth
Shamrock Shenanigans
Kitten Kaboodle
Costume Catastrophe
Candy Cane Caper
Holiday Hangover
Easter Escapade
Camp Carter
Trick or Treason
Reindeer Roundup

Hippity Hoppity Homicide
Firework Fiasco – *June 2018*

Zimmerman Academy The New Normal
Ashton Falls Cozy Cookbook

Tj Jensen Paradise Lake Mysteries by Henery Press:
Pumpkins in Paradise
Snowmen in Paradise
Bikinis in Paradise
Christmas in Paradise
Puppies in Paradise
Halloween in Paradise
Treasure in Paradise
Fireworks in Paradise
Beaches in Paradise – *July 2018*

Whales and Tails Cozy Mystery:
Romeow and Juliet
The Mad Catter
Grimm's Furry Tail
Much Ado About Felines
Legend of Tabby Hollow
Cat of Christmas Past
A Tale of Two Tabbies
The Great Catsby
Count Catula
The Cat of Christmas Present
A Winter's Tail
The Taming of the Tabby
Frankencat
The Cat of Christmas Future

Farewell to Felines
The Cat of New Orleans – *June 2018*

Writers' Retreat Southern Seashore Mystery:
First Case
Second Look
Third Strike
Fourth Victim
Fifth Night
Sixth Cabin – *May 2018*

Rescue Alaska Paranormal Mystery:
Finding Justice
Finding Answers – *May 2018*

A Tess and Tilly Mystery:
The Christmas Letter
The Valentine Mystery
The Mother's Day Mishap

Sand and Sea Hawaiian Mystery:
Murder at Dolphin Bay
Murder at Sunrise Beach
Murder at the Witching Hour
Murder at Christmas
Murder at Turtle Cove
Murder at Water's Edge
Murder at Midnight

Seacliff High Mystery:
The Secret
The Curse
The Relic
The Conspiracy
The Grudge
The Shadow
The Haunting

Haunting by the Sea:
Homecoming by the Sea

Road to Christmas Romance:
Road to Christmas Past

USA Today best-selling author Kathi Daley lives in beautiful Lake Tahoe with her husband Ken. When she isn't writing, she likes spending time hiking the miles of desolate trails surrounding her home. She has authored more than seventy-five books in eight series, including Zoe Donovan Cozy Mysteries, Whales and Tails Island Mysteries, Sand and Sea Hawaiian Mysteries, Tj Jensen Paradise Lake Series, Writers' Retreat Southern Seashore Mysteries, Rescue Alaska Paranormal Mysteries, and Seacliff High Teen Mysteries. Find out more about her books at **www.kathidaley.com**

Stay up to date:

Newsletter, *The Daley Weekly* http://eepurl.com/NRPDf
Kathi Daley Blog – publishes each Friday
http://kathidaleyblog.com
Webpage – www.kathidaley.com
Facebook at Kathi Daley Books –
www.facebook.com/kathidaleybooks
Kathi Daley Books Group Page –
https://www.facebook.com/groups/569578823146850/
E-mail – kathidaley@kathidaley.com
Twitter at Kathi Daley@kathidaley –
https://twitter.com/kathidaley
Amazon Author Page –
https://www.amazon.com/author/kathidaley
BookBub – https://www.bookbub.com/authors/kathi-daley
Pinterest – http://www.pinterest.com/kathidaley/